SIT WITH IT

NOVEL 4 IN THE SERIES
SCRAPBOOKS OF THE SOUL

MARILYN HAMMOND, PHD

EMPRESS

PUBLICATIONS

WWW.EMPRESSPUBLICATIONS.COM

SCRAPBOOKS OF THE SOUL

Explore the mesmerizing universe of **Scrapbooks of the Soul**, a compelling series of novels where fiction merges with profound inquiry. Each book is a rich mosaic, filled with diverse fictional characters who delve into the mysteries of the soul, sleeptime dreams, brain hemispheres, and the intersections of spirituality and science. Their dialogues, embellished with insightful footnotes, navigate through themes of whole-brain Christianity, and the intricacies of psychological, generational, and cultural healing.

These stories are more than narratives; they are a reflection on human experience, encompassing long-standing friendships, resilient relationships, and our struggle with life's opposites. The series offers a unique perspective, suggesting our reality is shaped by our perceptions and interpretations. Engage with **Scrapbooks of the Soul** to discover a world where each page mirrors the complexity of life and the varied interpretations that define our existence.

DEDICATION

Loving gratitude to Holly for insightful, novel suggestions, related to the stories

TABLE OF

CONTENTS

CHAPTER ONE

Discernment

"Be kind to all you meet, for everyone carries a heavy load," ended the newspaper obituary of someone in his early twenties who'd killed himself. The beginning of the obituary had been upbeat, telling of this young man's talents, interests, and vitality. That's why the fact of suicide was shocking and the ending sentence of the obit sadly appropriate.

Dee Kendrick sat with this tragic information, stunned. His dying from Covid-19 would have made more sense, for the coronavirus was still raging. She sincerely desired peace for this young male she did not know, prayed for his family, friends, and all who knew him.

Dee was stricken to wonder whether she was suicidal at the very time she had the crucial invitation from Aunt Tess to live with her in Stamford. She remembered an evening she was devoured by loneliness, failure, fears, confusion. Loneliness was the worst, and Mister her dog may have saved her from total desolation and final destruction that evening. Then, Aunt Tess's note arrived in the mail a day or two later, and Dee said "yes" where times before she'd said "no" to moving to Stamford.

Dee looked back on the synchronicities of that time. How Aunt Tess had her own end-of-life desperations, and likely already had liver cancer but didn't know it. For the first time, Dee realized family bonds saved both of them through each other. Well, she knew that but not as fully as now, when social-distancing was increasing loneliness—a killer in its own way.

That evening, Dee showed Zach the obituary she found enormously sad, which they discussed. The fact of this young person's suicide as well the reality that everyone carries a heavy load and sometimes an extra heavy load as during the Covid pandemic. Zach agreed the obituary said more than most, and remembering his panic attack years ago knew the truth of acute psychological pain.

These November Covid-evenings in 2020, Zach and Dee no longer sat together in their dual recliner because of the virus, but apart in the family room, talking about the day's activities, especially' the polarized politics which brought exhaustion alongside the pandemic, but would hopefully lessen now that the 2020 presidential election was over.

They were set to watch the evening TV news when second-grade teacher, daughter Cynthia, living with them during the pandemic, appeared in the family room with canine Pixie-Pickett. Cynthia and her dog were inseparable. Indeed, the small Pekingese brought delight to the entire household.

Seeing Dee and Zach seated separately, Cynthia wondered why they were still sleeping together if no longer sharing the dual recliner, but didn't ask. She was becoming more restraint of tongue. Perhaps because of feeling more fulfilled with Merriweather school teacher Quinn Collins in her life, having friend psychotherapist Sherry in town as a casual sounding board, Cynthia was in a reasonably OK place psychologically though overwhelmed as a new teacher teaching online because of Covid.

Not knowing about the obituary Zach and Dee had been discussing, and hearing only about being kind to everyone you meet, Cynthia inserted, "I say be kind while discerning of everyone you meet, for not everyone is of good character, decent intention, and if all one has in the toolkit of life is an attitude and reaction of kindness, that would not be adequate to handle life's many situations."

Dee explained the obituary they'd been discussing and Cynthia agreed kindness was an appropriate sentiment in the obituary but not solely sufficient in everyday living. Cynthia was still working on being consistently kind with Dee, smashed with knowing how vulnerable she herself now felt teaching second graders online. Cynthia knew she would not do well without Quinn and Sherry at this time, plus the emotional and financial security she had living at home with Zach and Dee, able to save money when so many were facing financial fears; she'd begun contributing money to a food bank.

Just then, Cynthia's telephone rang in her room, whereupon she and Pixie-Pickett immediately left the family room to answer it, as Zach was saying he agreed with Cynthia's comment on the necessity of discernment, fully realizing Dee had made the word *discernment* a nuanced impactful household term, and complimenting Dee in Cynthia's absence, now talking on the telephone in her room.

Zach recalled that Dee had introduced the term 'discernment of spirits' from the spiritual exercises of St. Ignatius, which is discerning (distinguishing, discriminating) emotions and moods of consolation and desolation, pleasant and unpleasant, positive and negative. Zach remembered Dee had said some saint so-and-so believed discernment to be the most profound of all the virtues—he couldn't remember the name of saint so-and-so.

Zach was saying, "If only there was more discernment in today's radical polarizing politics; people at each end of the spectrum clinging to their extreme political positions at the corners rather than seeking cooperation in the spacious, generous center where there is the possibility of finding middle ground. Compromise is not weakness but cooperation for the common good."

Dee complimented him, as she'd done before, on his use of the human eye to illustrate political extremes in today's politics which continued to dominate news headlines even though the presidential election was now over. To Zach, "The healthy human eye has a wide range of vision, so how healthy is it to look only out of a corner of the eye politically, stuck in one corner or the other? The answer is obvious. It only makes sense to scan the entire range of viewpoints, opinions, possibilities, and seek creative compromise not out of weakness but out of understanding multiple credible points of view."

Dee remained impressed with Zach's metaphoric insight using the human eye to talk about the pitifully polarized political situation today. Amazingly, another profound metaphor having to do with community and creative conversation, had just entered her world.

CHAPTER TWO

Polyhedron

Dee showed Zach copies of internet images of polyhedrons as she care-

fully, teasingly forewarned, "What I am about to say may be a little too Catholic for you, however, I was reading Pope Francis's recent ninety-five page encyclical (letter) which he signed a month before the presidential election, at the tomb of St. Francis after saying Mass in the basilica in Assisi the hometown of St. Francis, last month on October 3, the day before St. Francis's feast day, when animals get blessed, on October 4.

"Pope Francis' long letter is titled "Fratelli Tutti" in Latin, meaning Brothers All, fraternal brotherhood, which is how St. Francis addressed the men in the religious order he started eight hundred years ago, today's Franciscans. In this recent long letter Pope Francis gives an answer to today's polarized politics for which you use the human eye—how we see political situations, communal issues, ways of legislating, solving human problems."

Zach jested, "The pope has been copying my Protestant wisdom?"

Having the pope's long letter in hand, Dee laughed, "Maybe. Or, more precisely, he presents his own solution to the problem you so wisely illustrate with the eye. Here in chapter six, paragraph 215 of "Fratelli tutti," he speaks of:

> . . . the many-faceted polyhedron whose different sides form a variegated unity . . . represent a society where differences coexist, complementing, enriching and reciprocally illuminating one another, even amid disagreements and reservations. Each of us can learn something from others.

Dee explained, "A polyhedron (paa·lee·**hee**·druhn) is a geometric figure with many faces or surfaces. The pope speaks of the many differing points of view that make up cultures today and how living is largely about developing the art of encountering another's point of view, frame of reference. He writes,

> The word "culture" points to something deeply embedded with a people, its most cherished convictions and its way of life. A people's "culture" is more than an abstract idea. It has to do with their desires, their interests and ultimately the way they live their lives. To speak of a "culture of encounter" means that we, as a people, should be passionate about meeting others, seeking points of contact, building bridges, planning a project that includes everyone. This becomes an aspiration and a style of life (Fratelli tutti, para. 216).

Dee extrapolated, "Pope Francis uses the word 'dialogue,' which might be called the art of conversation, that I see is different from debate where one is trying to win over another, win an argument, whereas dialogue is respectful sharing, exchanging a cacophony of ideas without fearing collapse into unwanted compromise which dilutes everything into a meaningless melting pot of ideas.

"Dialogue is informed, finely tuned conversation, incisive and insightful instead of a boxing match in which each fighter goes into his corner, comes out fighting, then returns to his corner momentarily to refresh, stop the bleeding, so to speak, hear a few words from his trainer, and then come out fighting again."

Dee was amused at her thoughts of boxing, *Ah, the name Dempsey, don't forget, after prize-fighter Jack Dempsey. What a nightmare, in ways.*

She calmly continued, "Dialogue is not about a knock-out punch. It's more about articulating and discerning. It's the art of allowing oneself to be stretched, to expand one's horizons, while being persuaded and dissuaded by varying ideas, allowing new directions, expanding viewpoints; evaluating other points of view as well as our own more clearly."

Zach was fascinated with the pope's use of a geometric metaphor just as he had found satisfaction with what could be illustrated about polarized politics using the human eye. He noticed Dee had discerned the polyhedron was a *solution* to cultural-political *differences* (she preferred the word *differences* rather than culture wars, battles, clashes). Anyway, he'd been pleased to discover the human eye as a metaphor, and now the pope's polyhedron, and he tied all of this to Dee's never-ending interest in practical hermeneutics; how we interpret our experiences, our existence.

Zach commented, "It seems you're always circling back around to practical hermeneutics. You say you haven't had a career. Well, I'd say you've certainly had an enduring passion, which hasn't brought you a monthly paycheck, but rather, allowed you to contribute richly to the lives of others who have profited from your passion of religious inquiry."

Dee could never forget that her hermeneutic curiosity began with Ann Dramm introducing Dee to metaphoric discernment, which is different from descriptive metaphor, a distinct difference first noted by Ann's friend Gabby and upheld by Matti, birth mother of Julia now in Clarksdale, KS, whom Dee met at Ann's Dramm's funeral. Julia would become co-grandmother of Dee's young grandson Monty in Clarksdale, when his parents, Kendal (daughter of Julia and husband Marco) married Charles (son of Zach and Dee.)

Dee reflected that Zach's comment about her circling back to practical hermeneutics was bigger than hermeneutics. Her whole life felt like a kind of circling back: from a bleak life in her hometown in Connecticut to aunt Tess in Stamford. After aunt Tess's death in Florida, Dee circled back from Stamford to Zach and the children in Sandshell. She circled back to an ever-present reminder of Ann Dramm through meeting Julia Montel at Ann's funeral, and then they became in-laws.

Dee's isolation after Zach's panic attack caused her to create a lasting circle of friendship in the Brunch Bunch. Covid-19 brought Cynthia back to the house where Dee could sense transformations in her relationship with Cynthia. Dee told herself she was perhaps overthinking this whole concept of circling back.

But certainly, one of the joys of the years had been the predictability of year-after-year spending Thanksgiving and Christmas with Monique and family. However, this Covid season, such would not be the case. Monique and family would stay home.

Grandson Monty and his parents were not coming to Sandshell for Thanksgiving in two weeks. Dee had not seen her mother, Paula, during these Covid months, though they'd texted and telephoned plenty. Dee expected Thanksgiving to have its own specialness, for Quinn and Sherry would join Dee, Zach, Cynthia, at the oversized table on the Kendrick patio for the Thanksgiving feast.

Quinn and Sherry each made the commonsense decision not to travel to be with their families. Strange as it might seem, living in the same town with mutual friend Cynthia, Quinn and Sherry had never met. Social-distancing because of the pandemic brought strangeness in countless ways, as Cynthia was to discover and re-discover.

CHAPTER THREE

Homeless Shelter

At first, Cynthia was fully delighted Sherry, along with Quinn and his dog Bios, would share Thanksgiving with the Kendricks. As days passed, a worry set in. Cynthia was concerned Quinn might be overly charmed by Sherry's natural glamour. Cynthia could talk with no one about her growing, gnawing, unease.

Listening to golden-oldies music, Cynthia heard Judy Garland sing, "Me and My Shadow," and though the lyrics didn't exactly apply to Cynthia's present distress, some of the lines fit: "Me and my shadow, Not a soul to tell our troubles to, All alone and feeling blue."

Cynthia had learned the psychological label "shadow" from Sherry, as those parts of our personality we are partially or fully in the dark about, which have a life of their own. Though we haven't willingly invited them, they're in us as mood, impulse, emotion, drive, uninvited phantasy (not to be confused with conscious fantasy such as a daydream, a consciously-willed imaginative undertaking).

Cynthia regarded phantasies as automatic reactions to threat of survival, whether psychological or physical survival. They are undercurrents of pushes and pulls going on inside us, remaining unnamed unless we pay attention and name them, which tends to reduce their potency.

Cynthia recognized she felt threatened by Sherry's physical attractiveness, and was also aware how much she didn't want to lose Quinn, though he wasn't the great romance of her life. But how could she be sure? Mask-wearing and social-distancing since meeting Quinn allowed for only the most casual indications of affection between Cynthia and him. Cynthia hated the pandemic with all her might at the moment. Yet, Cynthia had met Quinn because of the pandemic protocol at the animal shelter, having to wait outside the building in the sunshine, when she'd left her water bottle in the car.

And why did Cynthia value Sherry's attractiveness over her own? Cynthia reasoned to herself, *Some situations must be accepted at face-value. We're all vastly different from each other, down to fingerprints. I'll not waste time and energy on something I can do nothing about. I hate this kind of competition—comparison. I'm not letting these worrisome thoughts have their way with me. When they come, I'll simply remind myself I need not waste effort on the aggravation of comparing myself against others. We all, simply are, as we are.*

Sure, I know, another part of my personality will then taunt that I am in 'denial,' lying to myself to make myself feel better. So, I'll have to deal with that. And on goes our venture of dealing with ourself. Dee's explication of Jesus' parables makes dealing with our own personality 'a cross' we must carry. I agree with her.

Despite these vexations, Cynthia was eager for Thanksgiving, the traditional menu, hoping for rousing conversation, like that summer when Francine shared much at the patio dinners.

This Thanksgiving Day did not disappoint. An abundance of traditional food began being prepared on Wednesday by the Kendricks, with Quinn and Sherry bringing side-dishes on Thursday. The group did not eat their feast until mid-afternoon Thanksgiving, sitting generously spaced at the oversized patio table after the five of them helped distribute the noonday traditional Thanksgiving meal at a homeless shelter.

Having been at the shelter with tattered and torn folk, those who seemed abandoned by life's goodness, throw-away people, those who'd fallen through the cracks, it seemed natural the conversation at the table began with talk about Pope Francis' recent encyclical, "Fratelli Tutti," (Brothers All) that Dee and Quinn had read online.

Those who ate their Thanksgiving meal at the shelter today, were emotionally still with these at the Thanksgiving table on the Kendrick patio when Zach jokingly threw out a comment about, "A summary of the pope's lengthy encyclical," to which Quinn thoughtfully answered, "This isn't a summary, but what pops into my mind is the similarity between the pope using characters in the Good Samaritan parable to talk about characteristics in ourselves. He said something like, 'All of us have in ourselves something of the wounded man, something of the robber, something of the passers-by, and something of the Good Samaritan,' which I feel Dee did in a penetrating way throughout her explication of the parables and the human personality."

Psychotherapist Sherry complimented, "Dee did do that exceptionally well, I agree." Zach and Cynthia readily added agreement and Dee secretly offered immediate upbeat heartfelt thanksgiving, for their words *did her heart good—a strange psychological phrase, with possible physical heart implications,* she told herself.

Quinn tried to summarize the pope's letter, "The first part is about broken human relationships in today's world, individually, culturally, globally." Cynthia posed a question to Sherry, "If we could have heard the life-stories of the people eating today at the shelter, would we have heard mostly about a collection of broken relationships or bad choices?"

No one tried to answer Cynthia's question until Sherry remarked, "I'd say in psychotherapy it's usually a complex combination of both broken relationships and bad choices, plus other unfortunate circumstances. Actually, sometimes another person's bad choices, or inadequacies of one sort or another, mental/emotional unhealthiness in general takes its toll on the one who has been damaged. It's hard to say, though broken relationships and bad choices figure prominently in human dysfunction in general. Sometimes generational dysfunction or systemic societal ills are to blame. Maybe it's easier to describe what promotes mental/emotional health and well-being than to list all that can go wrong."

As Sherry gave her lengthy reply, Cynthia realized she may have been competing with psychotherapist Sherry posing the question of broken relationships or bad choices, perhaps to impress Quinn, or stymie Sherry in front of Quinn. Cynthia also realized she liked provocative questions. Maybe she was only wanting to provoke stimulating conversation. She told herself she was trying to be self-aware but not self-absorbed, and agreed completely with Dee's conclusion that the personality is a cross each of us bears.

Just then Dee began talking about the pope's letter being principally concerned with an increasing global economy while at the same time there is a growing globalized indifference of humans toward humans. "He said more than once we need to realize we are all in the same boat. He is promoting a culture of meaningful personal encounter to overcome the tendency to indifference."

Dee then offered, "I will play the role of the devil's advocate[1] challenging the pope's concern about indifference: TV news these days shows long lines of people at the airport waiting to travel home to family for Thanksgiving; so it seems to me family is cherished, celebrated in our world today.

"Also, because of the pandemic, TV presents scenes of cars lined-up, people getting food available from food banks. Food banks show that culture cares, as do large groups inside homeless shelters receiving meals, as was our experience today. Plus, Zach has long worked with affordable housing. Aren't these all indications of human caring? This doesn't look like human indifference."

Dee's talk of human caring triumphing over human indifference these days brought a cascade of random comments from the others, as if the experience at the homeless shelter put them into a rare mindset.

---

[1] Playing the devil's advocate means presenting a certain point of view you don't necessarily agree with for the sake of exploring a situation more fully. This practice was used within the Catholic Church where an appointed person presented arguments or evidence against canonization of a candidate so as to insure thoroughness of the process.

CHAPTER FOUR

Devil's Advocate

They played the devil's advocate as a group, creating a barrage of statements from the group:

"Traveling home to family may be altogether selfish with Covid raging, thus spreading the virus."

"Family is a vestige of tribalism."

"Family is the basic means of survival in any culture."

"Lines at food banks may be stark evidence of marginal-wage jobs and lives upended when the economy hiccups."

"The economic upheaval at this time is way more than a hiccup and hits far more than marginal-wage people."

"There is too much credit-card debt and every kind of debt, and thus not enough savings for an emergency."

"For an emergency that lasts month after month after month, like Covid? That's like saying people living in the Dust Bowl in the '30s should have saved enough money to last them year after year of the drought."

"People like us who help serve the homeless on Thanksgiving and Christmas may feel better about ourselves, but overall, why do we have a culture with so many homeless?"

"Because many homeless have mental problems and addiction problems. We will soon have a vaccine for Covid-19, but addiction can't be treated with a vaccine; recovery from addiction seems to require genuine human encounter, and who knows what else."

"After Covid has been vaccinated away, there will still be the opioid crisis, so why do we have so much addiction?"

"We're trying to fill holes in the soul."

"Minority groups are harder hit with the virus and economic devastation."

"Life isn't fair."

"That's merely a cliché."

"Cliches can have deep roots."

"If those with privilege were more aware, life would become more fair."

"There are huge private foundations of the mega-rich that do a wealth of good these days."

"The mega-rich get tax breaks with their foundations.

"Taxes on the wealthy should not be reduced."

"Even Jesus said there will always be poor people. It's just part of life."

"And there will always be rich people. They have a lot more than they need."

"Some people work harder than others."

"Some are more capable."

"Some are less capable, which may not be their fault."

"Some have more opportunities than others."

"The strong have to help those weaker. Help the weak learn how to be stronger."

"It's not always that simple."

"I believe life worldwide is getting better in the long run."

"Except when it's not, with increasing numbers of refugees from war, famine, desire to escape grinding poverty."

"It takes courage to leave one's country, one's culture, for a better life."

"And is life better for those in the new country to which they'd fled?"

"What exactly is a better life?"

"I'd say president Franklin Delano Roosevelt's four freedoms: 'freedom of speech, freedom of worship, freedom from want, freedom from fear' is one way to talk about a good life."

"Talk is cheap, making the ideal real is the hard part. Further, now with the internet, is freedom of speech necessarily ideal? If not, who should censor?"

"Though Roosevelt was speaking to his time, his day, there's something basically true about what he said."

"We should be able to learn from history?"

"The bible book of Ecclesiastes says 'All is vanity.'"

"Overall, I believe human behavior evolves towards the better."

"So why did the pope write this recent long letter?"

"It's part of his job description."

Everyone laughed.

"Will the Kingdom of God have arrived when Western culture dominates the globe?"

"Are you kidding? Western culture, which has birthed the holocaust, nuclear warfare and ecological distress?"

"Do you prefer non-science cultures?"

"They may have some advantages."

"Has the Kingdom of God been advanced by the United Nations?"

"That's a bizarre notion; incongruent. The Kingdom of God is a Christian way of speaking. The United Nations represents all nations, not just Christianized nations."

"Maybe the Kingdom of God is a strange notion. A strange, unattainable utopian idea which is valuable though unattainable."

"If only humans were wiser. We lack wisdom."

"Today, we have much information, little wisdom. How does someone become wise?"

"Maybe wisdom is a natural by-product of love and truth."

"The word *love* can devolve into a sappy kind of love. The word *compassion* is better, for it includes creative suffering, unavoidable suffering as a part of life."

"Wisdom may be connected to 'no pain no gain' in a spiritual, a psychological sense."

"Wisdom and discernment are first cousins."

This group stream-of-consciousness was perhaps brought about by their homeless shelter experience. The conversational intensity continued.

CHAPTER FIVE

Incriminating Conversation

Quinn was saying, "Pope Francis is not politically naïve, having been head of the Jesuit Order in Argentina during the atrocities under the authoritarian rule of Juan Peron, and having to navigate between saving lives without aiding and abetting the assassinations carried out by Peron's dictatorship.

"The 2019 movie, *The Two Popes*, tells of this time in Argentina and of the pope's conflicted role when he was a much younger Jorge Mario Bergoglio, before he took the papal title, Pope Francis. He obviously admires St. Francis of Assisi. As a Jesuit, it seems more likely he would have become Pope Ignatius, but no, he's Pope Francis.

"I wonder if it was coincidence, or planned, that his "Fratelli Tutti" encyclical was released exactly one month before the U.S. presidential election, which coincided with St. Francis's feast day. Jesuit Bergoglio, having lived through Peron's reign of terror in Argentina could see destructive potential in our polarized politics and in tyrants and tyrannical politics in other parts of the world today.

"Early in the encyclical, he writes about a growing loss of the sense of history and how some ideologies flourish when people are ignorant of everything that came before them (para. 13). He questions, 'Nowadays, what do certain words like democracy, freedom, justice or unity really mean (para. 14)?'"

"Some might say releasing the encyclical on a date that highlighted both the saint's feast day and the upcoming U.S. presidential election, was coincidental, accidental, happenstance, or more importantly a twist of fate, a synchronicity, as Cynthia has taught me the word synchronicity.

"If releasing his encyclical was purposely tied to both Francis's feast day and our presidential election, I'd call that wise planning, wisely seizing a timely opportunity, delivering his document about the state of the world today; on one hand tied to the story of St. Francis who was known to have a generous attitude to those of religious persuasions different from his. St. Francis was about an all-consuming love of everybody, everything, including the sun, moon, nature itself. A tremendous kind of connectedness."

Dee, having written about St. Francis, was thinking to herself, *We must remember, it is not known that Francis of Assisi and his father were ever reconciled. Maybe it's easier to love nature than one's father. Perhaps. I wonder if the father-child relationship is so wrought with peril that Judeo-Christianity compensates for this with God as always and ever-Loving Father, even while also a stern father, handing down commandments and such.*

Dee was thinking of her own story; her father's expectations, which were not evil, yet not healthy for her. Dee and her father had never been estranged. They never had a conversation about why she was damaged by his expectation that she be tough Dempsey. Yet, as she understood more about his sick baby sister Agnes who died, the dynamics that drove him were clear and even made sense, though they were not good for Dee, except that she came to have compassion and respect for transgender issues, while not agreeing with all of today's physical remedies for the very real conundrum, which she had found to be more psychological than physical.

Zach had found his own father problematic, and he was beginning to understand that Cynthia felt overwhelmed and undone by his teasing which she was too young to understand, and which he exacerbated by joining in antics with Charles, leaving her feeling left-out and uncertain. Sure, kids are resilient, but they're also sensitive. Survival demands they be sensitive to what is going on around them. So, think how great is the damage done to the psyches, the souls of the victims of pedophilia. Does Church leadership really comprehend this at its fullest?

Dee was silently processing, *Human personality at its soul-depth is the core of most everything. I use the word soul rather than heart. We know heart is an organ in the body. Soul is not material-physical but an abstract essence said to animate, enliven the body, which lives on after death.*

Soul is our aliveness, our potential, that can be damaged as well as healed. Overlapping circles creating a mandorla show soul as a grand mix, a combustion chamber of transcendent and human qualities, between heaven and earth.

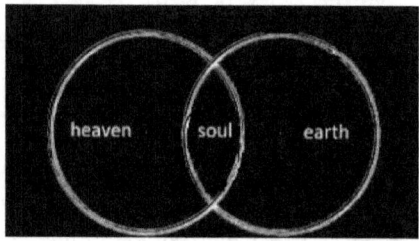

Quinn was again talking about Pope Francis, "He's 84 years old, having lived as an adult in Peron's tyranny. Putting all of this together, I see Pope Francis as an elderly person having the courage to say what he is certain needs to be said, and the Covid pandemic which has turned everyday life upside in many respects, is an optimal time to do this."

The vigor of the conversation was satisfying, political opinions intense, animated back and forth exchanges of fact and conjecture, which felt really good. Then, a pause in their talk made them aware in the momentary quiet that Bios was snoring. This amusing change in noise level awakened Pixie-Pickett. The shift in group dynamics caused the group to begin clearing the table, putting food away while watchful of the two dogs underfoot. The five adults made for a quick clean-up, and then dessert was enjoyed at the patio table with everyone again wearing masks after dessert, along with jackets in the evening coolness.

Talk turned to another recently released Vatican report: Four-hundred pages telling the story of a charming cleric elevated through the ranks of hierarchy eventually to the position of a Cardinal, while engaged in sexual abuse for years. The report covers what church leaders knew about his sexual activities and how the Cardinal denied such charges. The report, ordered by Pope Francis, in 2018, was to "follow the path of truth wherever it may lead."

Everyone at the Kendrick patio table knew a bit about the report and contributed to the talk about the need for transparency, as it was on TV news and in newspapers, and affirming again necessity for freedom of the press to counteract the human tendency to cover-up, wanting to hide, going back to Adam and Eve in the Garden, to control what is reported, whether that's a corporation covering its tracks, or an institution of any sort, including a religious institution.

The group fully acknowledged everyone wants to protect reputation, status quo, and can be reluctant to let be known even honest mistakes, resistant to exposing weaknesses, shortcomings, and certainly hiding atrocity.

The group knew basically the Vatican report found that the cardinal lied to his superiors about his pedophile atrocities, and some chose to believe him. It has been said Pope John Paul II having lived in Poland under the communist regime where clergy were falsely accused of sexual misconduct to discredit the Church, may have caused that pope to disregard sexual abuse reports about the cleric, and made him a Cardinal in 2001. Then, under Pope Benedict XVI, no action was taken against the cleric, as if all was well.

However, Pope Francis kicked the cardinal out of the priesthood in early 2019. His title becoming simply "Mr". He was sent to a remote Franciscan friary where he lived for a little over a year, but left there, and no one seems to know where he now lives. He's old, he'll die, and that's how it will end. But, of course, should all the priest pedophiles die tomorrow, the damage to their victims, victims' families, acquaintances, as well as damage done to the natural human quest for loving transcendent experience, will not easily be healed.

It's as if a rock has been tossed into stagnant waters far and wide splashing on innocents and innocence. What are the stagnant waters into which The Rock of Peter has thrown itself? Too many males at the helm of Holy Mother the Church? Too much reliance on left-hemisphere instruction without enough right-hemisphere inspiration, mystical experience, psychological connection to oneself?

Clerics vying for privilege rather than serving the needs of others? Lack of soul discernment, soul wisdom, practical personal hermeneutics including metaphoric discernment and symbolic discernment, coming to know oneself? Lack of being in touch with profoundly deep parts of soul (psyche), such as sleeptime dreaming?

Dreams are valued in both Hebrew and Christian scripture. Fear of Gnosticism is no defense against shallow, superficial ignorance or laziness about one's own deep soul. The church can be hyper-aware of the inadequacies of secular culture while blind to its own deficiencies, the need for its own institutional wisdom. Today's disenchantment with church culture is much the fault of church culture itself. Where is wisdom in the church, though books of the bible say a great deal about wisdom, referred to as "her, she."

CHAPTER SIX

Uncomfortable Cynthia

Cynthia offered a possibility, "What if priests now in prison for pedophilia would donate their brains after death to scientific research to see what might be learned. A group of nuns have designated their brains after death become part of research on dementia.

"What is unique with the nuns as a research group is the extensive records kept from the beginning of each becoming a nun. If such records are true for priests, then this could be a situation ripe for research. There would be all these records.

"With the nuns there was found a possible tie between idea density and dementia in late life. Idea density is the average number of ideas expressed per ten words. In looking at essays the nuns wrote when young, it was concluded that lower linguistic ability (idea density) in young adulthood seemed to pair with the risk of dementia in late life."

Sherry gently reviewed Cynthia's suggestion, "There may be a glitch in what you suggest with offending priests. First, dementia was studied with the nuns and dementia. Dementia isn't a criminal or moral offense, which pedophilia is both, so you may not get many volunteers for a brain study on pedophilia. Also, I doubt you'd have enough priests in prison for pedophilia to make up a research group, whereas all nuns of the one particular religious order were eligible to be part of brain research upon death if they so designated.

"Pedophiles often deny their sexual behavior, sometimes blaming their victims for enticing them, so with their strong denial, I doubt you'd find many volunteering their brains after death. However, even as we speak, researchers may be in contact with pedophiles in prison trying to understand the disorder." Cynthia agreed with Sherry's observations.

Then, Quinn took the conversation in a whole new direction, possibly to take any sting out of Cynthia's suggestion for research having been dismantled by Sherry. He was protective of Cynthia. Seemingly disconnected from anything just said, he introduced, a new topic, "I am attracted to a passage in the bible which is probably part of my love for the ancient Greeks.

"It's where the apostle Paul is in Athens at the Areopagus saying, 'You Athenians, I see you are very religious, for as I walked around looking carefully at your shrines, I even discovered an altar inscribed, To An Unknown God (Acts 17:22).'

"However much humans believe they know God, I disagree. I favor instead Isaiah 55:8 who has God saying, 'My thoughts are not your thoughts. My ways are not your ways.' I am very fond of the ancient Greeks and want to believe they were smart enough to know what they didn't know, and so they had this shrine to An Unknown God. They may have had other motives for building the shrine, but I prefer my explanation.

"Of course, the Greeks developed much that blossomed throughout western culture: theater, mathematics, science, philosophy, democracy, reason and intellectual inquiry into topics such as truth and beauty. When I'm overwhelmed, I find comfort in An Incomprehensible God; Creative Incomprehensibility."

Sherry agreed with Quinn's statement of his fondness for an Unknown God, by saying she preferred the idea of the Holy Spirit over that of the Father. "A male God has less appeal for me. Holy Spirit as genderless entity is more meaningful. While I respect Jewish monotheism was male, and Jesus gave us the Lord's prayer, the "Our Father," there is the Holy Spirit which seems a broader, greater, more comprehensive, less complicated way of looking at Being Itself."

Sherry added, "According to Japanese novelist Shusaku Endo (1923-1996), who wrote the novel, *The Life of Jesus*, the four most dreadful things are fires, earthquakes, thunderbolts, and fathers. I don't understand his statement and can't say I agree with it, however, I would not want God to be Mother as Being Itself, either—God as totally female. I believe religion is a turn-off for many today because it hasn't been sufficiently rethought for this time. Tradition can preserve history but also be repressive; even oppressive. I prefer God as Being Itself, genderless, or at least androgynous.

"Dee has had the courage to update fourfold exegesis for use today. She has taught us about parameters of metaphor, including the possibility that humans may not realize they are speaking metaphorically, as when speaking of God as Father. I know some today prefer to think of God as energy, essence, or Being Itself, which is my preference."

Cynthia was remembering Quinn told her of his preference of God as Being Itself, which his comment about the Athenian "Unknown God" seems to confirm. So, Quinn and Sherry were in agreement. Cynthia also noticed Sherry's compliment of Dee. It seemed Sherry was spreading her wings over the conversation, the gathering, and Cynthia felt discomforted.

Cynthia hoped Sherry didn't forget she was in Sandshell this Thanksgiving with Cynthia's family, having Kendrich family friend Francine as mentor, fortunate to be living in a beach apartment with a present and future livelihood coming to pass, all because of Cynthia—Cynthia's connections—Cynthia's caring for Sherry.

All this made possible for Sherry by Cynthia who was beginning to feel physically ill.

CHAPTER SEVEN

The Book of Revelation

Sherry was obviously enjoying herself, the group, the conversation. She began a new topic: the strange bible book of Revelation to John which she and her minister father had spoken about more than once.

John's phantasmagoric writing ends the Christian bible, and the question which intrigued Sherry is *why*? Why would or should this unusual book be the last book after Christians kept the whole of Hebrew scripture, added their own writings about Christ, and then ended with John's revelation. Why was it the last word, the final word, so to speak? She wondered about that.

Sherry continued her questioning, "Was John who wrote Revelation, a Seer, a visionary who saw complex, convoluted visions, or was he using a literary device, complex allegory to tell a story? In either case, what John tells is a tale of kaleidoscopic cosmic war, about Jesus the Christ as divine warrior, triumphant in time and history.

"The seven churches John evaluates were real churches in Asia Minor which John well knew, and can be found on a map of his day in the general area of the island of Patmos where John had been exiled by officials of the Roman Empire who used the island as a penal colony."

Quinn interrupted Sherry, "My sister and I visited Patmos, the exact cave where John supposedly lived during his exile. I have a tiny wood cross I bought there. We were typical tourists, viewing the sights. Sorry to butt in."

Though not feeling well, Cynthia was trying to appear OK, asking the question, "What had John done to offend the Roman Empire?"

Sherry replied, grateful for her father's knowledge and sharing, "Apparently, it was almost impossible to share in a city's public life without taking part in the Roman Empire imperial cult. One could be faced with economic sanctions, be expelled from trade guilds, suffer the loss of property, or imprisonment. John likely resisted officials, official policy of the Roman Empire, or encouraged other Christians to resist, and gotten crosswise with people in power, so he was silenced through exile, except that on the island of Patmos he wrote the "Apocalypse of John" which ends the bible, so he wasn't silenced, he hasn't been silenced, not to this very day. John's apocalypse (revelation) is read today, but, oh my, how the book of Revelation has been interpreted—through the ages and even today!

"Most recently my father has shared that just as each of the Four Gospels paints a portrait of Jesus the Christ, John's book of revelation is another portrait of Christ Jesus, a fifth portrait—as triumphant cosmic entity—victor over all else—such as lesser points of view, collective mindsets, societal standards, hardships, misunderstandings.

"John paints this portrait of triumphant Christ Jesus to encourage followers in the hard times they were going through butting heads with the Roman Empire. Perhaps the revelation to John ends scripture because whenever there's turmoil, trouble, stress, seemingly insurmountable difficulty, this fifth portrait of Jesus reassures and comforts struggling humanity that Christ is victorious throughout the universe, the cosmos—always and ever—whatever the circumstances on earth.

"John uses earthquakes, falling stars, hail, locusts, frogs, the Four Horsemen, the Number of the Beast, the battle of Armageddon, the lake of fire that burns with sulfur, the thousand-year reign, the second death, to tell his story.

"I'm interested in the book of Revelation as a story about the struggles of the human soul, the psyche, the psychological world, often referred to in the bible as the 'heart.' Christ is victorious over our external fears, the terrors of our age, stupidities and vanities that sometimes surround us, or meaningless answers given to profound questions, people and situations who annoy and complicate our lives.

"The Revelation to John can encourage when we suffer with internal fears, troubles, overwhelming perplexities, unrealizable hopes, personality problems that vex us about ourselves, the longing to know ourselves, find our Infinite path, and be guided along that path. Victorious Christ is available as cosmic companion as John's story reveals.

"My father taught me a most valuable lesson about the power of praise, and there's a fair amount of praise in John's cosmic revelation. Dee has mentioned St. Francis praising when he was knocked-down by life. I have found praise a faithful companion when I'm overwhelmed. I willfully, purposely, mentally extol profuse words of admiration, paying tribute, thanking, adoring, exalting, acclaiming that which IS above all else. I do believe there is Ultimate Isness, Being Itself—the Beingness of the universe—which to me is the most awesomely profound reality and possibility in the exterior universe—and in my personal universe—and I praise this entity with reckless abandon, thanking, adoring, uttering words I wouldn't say in front of another human. Praise somehow diminishes my disturbing situation, puts my problems in perspective.

"This kind of praise is psychologically sound. While Being Itself doesn't need praise, my lavish acknowledgement of Being Itself puts puny me in a different psychological place. My little corner of the world changes. I'm like a chick being hatched out of my confining shell, bursting forth into a larger psychological framework, a bigger world of Being.

"Some may find Being Itself too imprecise, too indefinite. I dismiss this objection, for in Alcoholics Anonymous Twelve Steps the term "Higher Power" is imprecise but effective without being irritating. When the Twelve Steps were being put together, finding a workable term for most people wasn't easy to do, until the label "Higher Power" was adopted.

"In Revelation John's mind, the term "Higher Power" would likely have been regarded as pagan, heretical, heathen or somehow unacceptable. We are living in a different age, where Pope Francis encourages polyhedron conversation, which I find compatible with Quinn's mention of the Athenian shrine to "An Unknown God." I tend to prefer open-endedness to closure in many instances. I find new horizons energizing for the most part.

"I find the term "Higher Power" inclusive the way Paul was in Galatians 3:28, "There is neither Jew nor Greek, slave nor free, male nor female, for you are all one in Christ Jesus." Now, we could perhaps have a polyhedron conversation about St. Paul's comment. I do believe some ideas are richer than others, and therefore appreciate Pope Francis's suggestion of polyhedron conversations, although there are bound to be downsides there, too. Everything has a shadow-side. I see this ever more clearly, just as shadows are part of everyday physical existence."

"For instance, I have enjoyed this time together so much I've been talking far too much, and therefore I apologize. That's a down-side to my present enthusiasm—a shadow element. Yet, I want to make one more comment. Cynthia has astutely observed recently a vaccine will eventually solve the Covid problem, however, a vaccine will not unscramble the opioid crisis. More factors are involved. I think again of the term "Higher Power," as a way to access 'grace' to overcome addiction and build back lives.

"I suggest abstract theological arguments will not be of much help healing the opioid crisis unless such arguments are distilled into something that works for everyday people. I believe Cynthia's observation about the complexity of the opioid problem is one of wise assessment. And Dee, your use of the word "exponential" is helpful. I feel we must move past black/white thinking (duality) to exponential processing, such as your fourfold interpretation of the parables."

Zach, having a tendency to pick-up on Cynthia's discomforts, added, "Pope Francis's recent encyclical deals with how this age is flooded with information compared to having sparse wisdom, and wisdom is going to be needed to solve the opioid pandemic." Zach was giving Cynthia credit for having been the first person he'd heard talk about something more than a vaccine would be needed to deal with the opioid crisis.

Cynthia's sensitivity at the moment was acute coupled with feeling physically worse and worse. She didn't want anyone to rescue her. She wanted Sherry to over-talk more than she already had, and thus said, "Sherry, I wish you'd say more about everything having a shadow-side."

Sherry complied though feeling she'd already talked too much, "I'll tie the shadow-side to Satan in John's Revelation where there's a fair amount of talk about Satan being conquered. I'll try to be coherent and concise."

CHAPTER EIGHT

Satan

Sherry began, "For life to be complete, all things must be potentially possible, everything must have its opposite plus all gradations in-between. I notice Revelation John's absolutes in his ancient writing. For him, nothing is gray, so to speak, everything is black or white. I would say this was John's hermeneutic, having learned to appreciate hermeneutics from Dee. Perhaps some say we live in an age of relativism, which has its shortcomings, but absolutism also has its shortcomings. That's what is meant by everything having its shadow-side; an unforeseen glitch, a downside, a side-effect, a not-ideal by-product, an unintended consequence.

"There's a good-bit about Satan in John's Revelation. My small mind has concluded that for Life to BE, everything must potentially exist—every positive has a potentially negative opposite, just as every potential negative has a positive—opposites exist—opposites simply ARE—intrinsically part of Beingness Itself; Total Being.

"We humans must choose between this and that. Instead of love there is hate or indifference, and vice-verse. The opposite of wisdom is perhaps stupidity, inadequate understanding, insufficient discernment, lack of subtle knowing.

"To me, Satan epitomizes, encapsulates, is the sum total of traits or qualities that stifle, maim, diminish Life as it is played out in human choices. John attempts to describe fully evolved Messiah Jesus' (fully human, fully divine) triumph over strangulating decisions humans make. Human personalities generate Life-defeating or Life-promoting agendas, which I appreciate as Dee's moral/choice category in her explication of Jesus' parables.

"I find John's Apocalypse attempts to explain Jesus' messianic victory over Satanic wrongness, not rationally, but through symbolic imagery, whether from his own spontaneous visionary experiences, or by intentionally writing with symbols.

"I suggest John also shows human error, expecting Christ to return soon and make everything OK. Now, almost two thousand years later, with hindsight we can look back and say John interpreted Christ's return incorrectly. He would have been more correct to have championed Grace, the workings of the Holy Spirit through humanity as Christ working through humanity to bring the Kingdom of God, and make life on earth better.

"Perhaps that is why John's book ends the bible—why it's the last word, so to speak. First, it's an obvious lesson in not interpreting literally, but rather, an intensive course in symbolism. Second, it's a clear case that Jesus wasn't teasing when he said he didn't know when the end of the world or time would come—not even the angels know that. Yet, from time to time, humans think they've got this figured-out, and get all fearful and freaked-out.

"Quite possibly John's cosmic tale ends the bible to help humans steer clear of being too literal when they read the bible, and too cocksure they know the future. The lesson is to live fully in the present with Grace, whatever the circumstances.

Sherry concluded, "Thanks, Cynthia, for your question about the shadow-side of life. My answer to your question has temporarily helped me understand the question *why* John's book ends the bible. And thank you Cynthia, for this Thanksgiving, and for all you have brought into my life in the time I've known you."

Cynthia was now too sick to continue caring about the conversation. Her chest was heavy, she ached all over and felt feverish. She didn't want anyone to know how miserably sick she was, as she nodded in Sherry's direction, acknowledging Sherry's thanks.

Quinn was just then saying the books of Ezekiel and Daniel in the bible are apocalyptic, which in Greek means "to uncover," "to reveal." Apocalyptic literature is about otherworldly journeys told by angels or in dreams or visions, where secrets of cosmic happenings are revealed.

Cynthia had an observation worth sharing, but had not the energy to explain that in Dee's explication of Jesus' parables, the fourth (spiritual category) could have been turned into a cosmic story such as John's book of revelation, but Dee instead spoke in more earthly terms, not turning to cosmic speculation. To Cynthia, the book of Revelation sounded like science fiction. Phantasmagoria. Today's Super Heroes, Action Figures.

No one suspected how sick Cynthia was.

CHAPTER NINE

Religion's Shadow

Quinn was animated by Sherry's ideas, "If you wanted to boil your version of Christianity down to its bare-minimum what three things would you keep, excluding the Trinity."

She answered immediately, "I'd say, Jesus, Grace and Holy Spirit. I wouldn't have included the Trinity, which has never been relevant to me. I've asked my dad for explanations, but nothing he or anybody else has offered makes the Trinity vital to me. Perhaps you have a convincing version of the Trinity?"

Quinn didn't respond to her question about the Trinity, "You wouldn't include John's Apocalypse in your three components?

Sherry said, "I would not include John's Apocalypse."

Sherry returned, "What three elements would you include?"

Quinn laughed, "I don't know. I've never thought of the question until now. I suppose I'd take it down to just one item—to Jesus. Everything else is to figure out who he was and is. You need Hebrew scripture to know who was the long-awaited Messiah by the Jewish people. Then, you need Christian scripture to tell about this One Hebrew Male, Jesus, thought by some to fulfill the Jewish expectation, why some people of his day decided he was the One, how they interpreted his life story, (especially Paul of Tarsus) which came to be written down, including the cosmic version in the book of Revelation. I add to that, my own exposure to His Story tied to my life experience."

Sherry summarized, "It seems to me I did that in my answer of three: Jesus, Grace, Holy Spirit. Why do you think many today when asked about their religious preference, answer "none." Perhaps they are rejecting the question, saying their religious preference is nobody's business. However, other numbers say church attendance is way down, so there are likely many today who do not have a religious affiliation."

Quinn summarized, "I'd say sex scandals in the Catholic Church, and 9/11 which at its core was international religious terrorism, are two major religious turn-offs for people today. And by the way, far back in history, the idea of the Trinity was a hair-splitting argument and church-splitting factor; a cause that possibly helped lead to the Great Schism of 1054. One Latin word *filioque,* which means "and from the son," helped finalize the split between Eastern and Western Christianity. Do you see why I am fond of the Athenian shrine to "An Unknown God." Humans putting too fine a point on what God IS, seems not a good idea.

"In today's world, our relationship with God may need to be less pre-determined and more free-flowing. Today, God as creative energy of the universe makes more sense, is more real than God as a Father-figure. Today, sexual impropriety, when found to be psychologically fragmenting or otherwise detrimental to one's life, one's overall well-being, mental/emotional state, may be more naturally avoided than fear of God's punishment will keep one chaste. However, one may not be aware of interior incongruencies. Socrates urged, "Know Thyself." Jesus spoke of inner peace."

Quinn seemed lost in his own thoughts while sharing, "Celibate clergy may not be qualified to talk against birth control. I'd say social justice is more important today than being God-fearing. Today, compassion may be more alive on a broader scale than ever before, which doesn't mean greed and cruelty, corruption and selfishness, many unsolved issues aren't still around.

"Religion must evolve. Institutional religion today must see its own sins, its own shortcomings, where it's stuck in its own development, its shadow-side, according to Sherry."

When Quinn spoke Sherry's name an emotional shudder went through Cynthia compounding her physical ailment, as she announced, "Sorry, everybody, I don't feel well. Please excuse me. My body aches, my chest feels heavy, no part of me feels OK. I'm going to bed." The thought, *Covid,* shot through everyone's mind as Cynthia left the patio into the house.

Cynthia, in her weakened state, vaguely realized it was a bit past 9:00 p.m. It was Thanksgiving. Where could she get medical help? Stumbling into bed, she knew her dad and Dee would see to it she was cared for. Of that, she was confident.

CHAPTER TEN

Cynthia's Diagnosis

Momentarily, Zach and Dee were at Cynthia's bedside. Yes, she had a fever a thermometer disclosed. Her parents gave her an over-the-counter medication to reduce fever and aching. Cynthia had rarely been ill, in general good health, only 25 years old, she could survive Covid, she dimly told herself. But where would she have contacted the virus? She'd been so careful. What if she'd given it to her parents, to Quinn and Sherry? They needed Covid tests. Cynthia had a heavy chest, but wasn't having trouble breathing. Maybe she didn't have Covid, she hoped.

Dee packed a small bag of essentials for Cynthia while there was a choppy exchange about Cynthia, too ill to speak, going to a hospital emergency room. Covid on the scene magnified everything. Then, the three of them were in the car on the way to a hospital emergency room where Cynthia was admitted, while Zach and Dee were told they could not enter the hospital to be with Cynthia who was assigned a bed, had vital signs taken, given a test for Covid.

Making sure Cynthia had her cell phone and charger, Zach and Dee parked awhile at the hospital hoping for a phone call. Zach was frozen in fear—his old buddy fear—exacerbated by the always-reality of Roxanne's death. Roxanne, still young, thought to be in mostly good health when she died.

The number of Covid deaths daily on the TV screen with the lives of a few detailed, made death exceptionally real these days. Plus, Zach did not forget his panic attack on a past Thanksgiving night. He knew the terrors of fear and was grateful Dee was fully functioning at this moment.

Waiting in the parking lot with no contact from Cynthia or hospital personnel, Dee and Zach finally drove home making the decision they would sleep with street clothes on, should they receive a call to come to the hospital hopefully to pick-up Cynthia and bring her home with medications for a more treatable malady than Covid. Dee covered the fully-made bed with a sheet and they slept atop the sheet with their clothes on, waiting for the telephone to bring good news.

They awakened early next morning, and shortly thereafter the telephone brought Cynthia's welcome voice saying the Covid test indicated she did not have the virus. She would call when she had more to report. Was it pneumonia? they wondered. The Covid teaching year had indeed been difficult for Cynthia. She was sorely disappointed the job in the Kansas City area fell through. Her immune system was compromised from prolonged stress, they concluded.

At breakfast, Zach was talking about himself, which was not usual for him. Why did he have such intense fear reactions? He'd obviously thought about this, and didn't want to be self-pitying, yet thoroughly honest. Was he simply "wired" that way? He'd had a stable childhood. Yet, his father's fears had been an ongoing part of the household. He continued, "Which makes me wonder if babies are like sponges picking up parents' emotions, continuing as toddlers and so on, soaking up what parents may not know about themselves.

"These pre-verbal feelings to babies are perhaps pockets of energy, transmissions so commonplace they are normal, routine, not questioned, just the way things are. And so it goes, year after year, growing up, generation after generation. We are even taught to be God-fearing, which I very much reject. Instead, we need to be taught God-healing, in awe of Incomprehensible Being, which Jesus epitomized."

Dee could certainly relate to soaking-up the emotional states of parents, as her confused gender issues taught her. She was thinking about last night's conversation about the book of Revelation and how frightening it is if you don't know it's not to be taken literally for this time or as future events coming to pass. Whether it's a style of writing, a genre of literature, a kind of imaginative cosmic speculation, or if it is a psychological vision, then, like a dream, it is to be regarded symbolically, metaphorically, not literally. After explicating Jesus' parables, she saw this more clearly than she had before dealing with the parables in a fourfold way.

Dee asked, "Do you agree with what Sherry laid out last night that humans choosing between 'Opposites' defines both wisdom and evil. That is, collective and individual wisdom comes from creative choices, and collective as well as individual evil comes from destructive choices and their consequences. Sherry's ideas about this made Dee reflect on what she did with Jesus' parables and the category of morality, wherein she did speak of the importance of the choices we make and their consequences.

Dee asked, "So, do you think there's a Devil, Satan, or such, or do those titles simply embody the accumulated effects of bad human choices?"

Zach reflected, "I've thought about the Nazis in World War II. Were they in the clutches of the Devil? Or, were there hateful decisions upon more hateful, destructive, catastrophic decisions until that collective mindset ruled in Germany? I'm inclined to believe it was all about human choices. When destructive ideas and actions begin to gain dominance, then creative ideas and actions fall by the wayside. Then, a fateful contest is going on. But it's not fate in the usual preordained sense, and yet a situation can come to seem fated.

"I don't think a devil or satanic power is needed other than the accumulative destructive power of human choice to create evil. My idea of looking out of only the corners of the human eye, as in political extremes, illustrates unwholesomeness. Inability to see the whole situation, can take one down an ill-fated path.

"Do I thus believe God is the accumulative creative power of wholesome human choices? In other words, do good human choices create God? No. It seems to me an already existing Creator is needed to create humans who will then be making choices. There's much I haven't worked-out. For instance, are tornadoes, earthquakes and such the evil side of Nature?

"I found last night's conversation interesting. I'm sorry Cynthia felt poorly and couldn't fully participate or enjoy what she had been looking forward to. Now that I look back on the evening, she was strangely quiet at times, which only made sense when she said she was sick and needed to go inside. I'm sad about that for her. She has fond memories of patio dinners with Francine."

Zach returned to the topic of fear as a destroyer of life, "However, fear can also cause one to take action to survive or to keep one from taking needed action. Fear isn't all bad, yet it certainly isn't all good."

Zach felt religion might be born out of fear—fear of death, fear of the process of dying, fear of annihilation. Less often, he felt religion might be born out of awe, praise, jubilation and wonder that we are alive and capable of asking *why, for what purpose are we alive?* "And we call Nature, Mother Nature. The Feminine. What does that have to do with Sherry's quote last night by the Japanese author who said, 'Four most dreadful things are fires, earthquakes, thunderbolts, and fathers.' So both fathers and mothers are at fault? If only children would be born without parents," Zach concluded cryptically.

It seemed to Zach that Dee had a fairly constant presence of Divine Providence. He told her that, and she said, "It's because I couldn't make it through life otherwise." She knew what was meant in the bible, "When I am weakest, then I am strongest." In touch with weaknesses, one can summon the strength of Christ. Dee did that.

Dee and Zach returned to talking about Cynthia as a first-time and online teacher; the stress she'd been under. They didn't know Cynthia's anxieties about Sherry and Quinn meeting, and wouldn't have suspected, for Cynthia had disclosed only friendship for Quinn. However, Cynthia's anxiety about Quinn and Sherry meeting was to have its own fateful twist.

CHAPTER ELEVEN

Monique and Chagall Paintings

Dee and Zach continued talking at the breakfast table, waiting for another phone call from Cynthia, as if their day couldn't begin until they heard from her. Dee spoke, "We've talked before about the need to return to an appreciation of *mythos*. Myth is not falsehood. Myth is merely a non-science, non-literal way to talk about Life."

"Sherry's comments on the book of Revelation in the bible as a fifth portrait of Christ, after the four Gospels, made me think of John's Revelation as a mythical version of Christ as cosmic entity. We do still have myth in culture with Super Heroes who have super powers. They save cities, come to rescue humans from danger.

"What humans also need is to be saved from psychological tragedy, battles of the soul, overwhelming fears and interior dilemmas that paralyze and destroy. Where we all really live is inside ourself in feelings, yearnings, longings, in confusion or with a sense of purpose. I plan to reread Revelation as a portrait of the transformation of the human person in Christ; the ultimate fulfillment of becoming the person we can be; as a mythological rendition of the interior life and attitudes; the treasure hidden in the field—a story of our soul, our psyche; soul healing; resurrection of what has been dead in us. I found uplifting Sherry's psychological praise of the act of praise."

Both Zach and Dee knew, without needing to saying so, they would not be able to talk so much about what Sherry contributed to last night's conversation in front of Cynthia. This would be deflating to Cynthia who had been too ill to contribute much.

Just then, the telephone brought a call from Cynthia happily saying she had been diagnosed with acute bronchitis and could now go home with appropriate antibiotics, and told them where to pick her up. What a relief.

Once home, Cynthia took to her bed, cozy and relieved with her treatable diagnosis. First, she slept a long time. Finally awake, she telephoned Sherry and then Quinn of her hospital stay, that she tested negative for Covid, was diagnosed with acute bronchitis. Zach and Dee were there to assure her comfort, address her every need and any whim that might arise. She felt loved, wonderfully cared for, indeed.

Zach telephoned Charles, Kendal and Monty in Clarksdale KS who were healthy and had had a most pleasant Thanksgiving with Kendal's parents Julia and Marc, Kendal's brother Patrick, wife Brooke, and baby girl Matti. The Sandshell group Zoomed with the Clarksdale group Thanksgiving afternoon, but today Zach was telling Charles about Cynthia now recovering in bed.

Charles and family met Sherry last Christmas, and zoom made it possible for them to meet Quinn this Thanksgiving. Dogs Bios and Pixie-Pickett were part of the Thanksgiving afternoon zoom call, which delighted toddler Monty, and may have mildly amused baby girl Matti. It was most gratifying to see the Montel family, so easy to have zoom contact on Thanksgiving with another nuclear family making them all extended family. Charles had done well to marry into the Montel family, already friends to the Kendricks.

That Thanksgiving weekend, Cynthia began to feel physically better, and was not yet burdened with classroom responsibilities, not until Sunday afternoon when young students again became her concern. Thankfully, it wouldn't be long before Christmas vacation was to begin, and this thought moderated her teaching concern which was about to be replaced with another concern of a far different kind, though she didn't yet know this.

Meanwhile, Monique telephoned Dee saying the Brunch Bunch members needed to meet before Christmas, either with a zoom meeting or on Dee's screened-in patio, which surely provided enough airflow to keep the coronavirus at bay. They met on the Kendrick patio.

Monique continued to be enthralled with the art of Marc Chagall, and had the huge Chagall book with her, citing page numbers from the book, "I begin to understand my enchantment with Chagall's work. He paints *unreason*, a peculiar hybrid symbolism which opposes the rationalized modern world.

"Like me—I am drawn to unreason. I can be unreasonable; I am unreasonable but with purpose. Chagall, born in Eastern Europe, fell in love with Paris when he arrived there. Me, too, born and raised outside Paris, I fell in with bright lights, colors, the people of Paris. Something broke inside me when Henri and I married against wishes of parents and came to the U.S. Chagall's lights and colors help put me back together, just like our group trip to Paris made me ache, ache terribly inside me, besotted with Paris, as Chagall was, and as his art is to me.

"His bright lights, intense colors, the light of liberty, liberation, yet, so too, the pigs and livestock on my grandparents farm. Paris holds the mystery of life, the stream of life, those strong, pure colors. His colors are primeval force, they vibrate. People's houses are primeval, too, vibrating life lived there, and so real estate speaks to me.

"And, get this" Monique showed them the painting The Wedding, 1910 in which, "The one side moon, feminine, and other side masculine, sun coloring. Like two hemispheres of the brain." Monique congratulated herself on making this connection between brain hemispheres and Chagall's painting by adding, "He paints years before brain-hemisphere research. His high intuition. He knew by intuition. His paintings on many levels."

She summarized, "His art is integration, of reality, union of soul and world, our miraculous existence. I see also in Estelle's icon of female tenderness. Paintings tell more than words. In dream images, too."

Monique's keen mind was again obvious to the group, as she ended, "Oh, I'm not finished with Chagall. There's more—much more."

CHAPTER TWELVE

Sherry and Quinn

Cynthia recovered from bronchitis and was again concerned about her young students. Before the first week after Thanksgiving ended, her pre-occupation became Quinn and Sherry. Cynthia was correct to suspect the two of them might "click." Quinn told Cynthia after Thanksgiving on the first day returning to walking the dogs to the park that he and Sherry had been talking on the telephone. He told how he first called Sherry to see if she'd heard anything about Cynthia in the hospital. The two had exchanged telephone numbers Thanksgiving night outside the Kendrick house as the Kendricks were getting ready to take Cynthia to the hospital, so whoever heard about Cynthia's condition first, would call the other.

Cynthia had mixed feelings about Quinn and Sherry. She couldn't afford to lose the friendship of either one. It wasn't easy to meet new people during the pandemic. She and Quinn had never verbally detailed their relationship, yet she had rather assumed they might become a pair, a couple of sorts. With Covid, everyone, everything was in a waiting-pattern. Sherry hadn't recently mentioned Justin, neither to indicate he was or wasn't in her life. But then, maybe Justin was gay after all.

Cynthia was fond of Quinn, his thoughtfulness, his range of interests, and his physical appeal. Sherry was, of course, very dear to Cynthia who wouldn't want to lose the friendship of either of Sherry or Quinn.

Cynthia telephoned Sherry that evening, "Quinn says the two of you have been talking. I'm glad," she added dishonestly. Yet, in a sense, Cynthia meant her comment, for Sherry knew very few people in town while Cynthia had grown-up there. She knew old classmates, people around town. Whereas Sherry knew mostly clients, and clients weren't likely to become friends.

Yet, Sherry's glamour had always intimidated Cynthia, and that's what was at stake now, being outshone by Sherry. Should Cynthia expect Quinn and Bios to continue to go to the park with Cynthia and Pixie-Pickett? It would be awkward for Cynthia to bring up the matter. She would simply remain flexible—let Quinn do all the navigating, while she followed his lead. Honestly, Cynthia had entertained slightly the idea of being married to Quinn—two teachers living on a Greek island during the summer, which seemed plausible, enjoyable, yet they never came close to talking about such. Should Quinn and Sherry become bonded romantically, Cynthia could see herself losing her two closest friends, stranded, alone and lonely. Then, she'd absolutely have to leave Sandshell—get out of town.

Neither Quinn or Sherry had been sneaky about their talking together. Did that mean romantic attraction was such they couldn't keep it a secret, or platonic-friendship was such there was no need to make it a secret. Cynthia wondered which was which. Should she tell Zach and Dee? Should she seek their advice on how to react? Cynthia did neither. She would wait-and-see, which was, after all, the order of the day with Covid.

Sherry planned to drive to Georgia to spend Christmas with her parents and siblings she hadn't seen in a long while because of Covid. Cynthia remembered Sherry meeting Justin last Christmas, their amusing dance through the kitchen, Sherry's intrigue with Justin, not knowing whether he was smitten with her.

Quinn would once again spend Christmas with another high school teacher at Merriweather and his family, which was what Quinn always did when he didn't go to family in Indiana.

After not spending Thanksgiving with the Kendricks, Monique and family would be with them this Covid-year Christmas, on the patio and in the backyard, including Christiane's fiancé Carter and his two daughters, slightly older than Christiane's five-year-old son, now again called Jameson, as he insisted, bonded to his father James in the wheelchair, who would also be at the Kendricks on Christmas. Would there be awkward moments when Christiane's ex-husband James, and Carter her future-husband, meet?

Christmas day, Monique commandeered the group's attention after everyone had eaten, as had become her custom. She'd brought her laptop computer, so as to share the video of an Episcopal priest delivering his sermon in Texas. Monique's dear friend, Dorothy in Dallas, a member of the Episcopal Church of the Transfiguration, alerted her to the online sermon. Monique had watched and listened to the sermon on Christmas Eve, bonded with it, and made the decision she would share it with everyone on Christmas Day. Which she did.

CHAPTER THIRTEEN

The Sermon Monique Brought

Christmas Eve Sermon – Perfect Companion – 2020

"A few weeks ago, a young man became an Ironman. I'm not talking about the fictional superhero in a metal suit, I'm talking about a very real young man named Chris Nikic who swam 2.4 miles, biked 112 miles, and then ran a full 26.2-mile marathon in one continuous race. Incredible, isn't it? By finishing under a certain time, Chris joined an elite group of athletes know as Ironmen.

"But Chris didn't become an Ironman alone. He raced with his coach, a man named Dan Grieb, who ran the entire course with him. Because, you see, Chris Nikic has Down Syndrome. Because of this, Chris needed a guide, someone to help him stay on course. It's a 16-hour grind on the racecourse, and it would be easy for anyone to miss a turn or get lost. So Chris' coach, Dan Grieb became his companion.

"In order to get him to the finish line, Dan couldn't coach Chris from a distance. He couldn't just give Chris techniques in advance, or train with Chris before the event and then cheer from the sidelines. In order to get Chris to the finish line, Dan had to be there, too. Which means, Dan was at Chris' side for every single inch of the 140 miles of swimming, cycling, and running.

"Moments before the race, Grieb told Chris' dad, "You've done an amazing job with your boy for 21 years. Just give him to me for (the next few hours) and I promise I'll return to you an Ironman." And after the race he told reporters, "The greatest honor of my life was keeping that promise."

"So, I guess I misspoke when I said that a young man became an Ironman a few weeks ago, didn't I. Because *two* people became Ironmen a few weeks ago. Chris . . . and his companion, his guide, his friend.

"Sometimes you just can't get there on your own. No matter how much you want to, no matter how hard you try, you just can't get where you want to go by yourself. Sometimes you need a companion, a guide, a friend. And with them by your side, racing all the long miles of the journey with you, you are able to accomplish more than you ever could have hoped for. Sometimes, in order to do something great, you need someone to do it with you.

"That's what Christmas is really all about. God wanted so much for us to get to the finish line, to reach our goal, to become (the righteous Ironmen and women) who we were always meant to be, that God decided to run every last mile of the race with us. Cheering from the sideline wouldn't be enough. To get us there, we would need someone at our side. So, God sent us the perfect companion, guide, and friend, his very own Son, so that we would know the way and stay on course. We'd still have to run our own race of life, but we wouldn't have to do it alone. He'd be there every step of the way.

"This kind of sacrificial solidarity, this kind of costly companionship, is what we mean when we say that love came down at Christmas. Only love can explain why God would choose to enter into our weak and weary world. God could see the suffering and pain of all creation, weighed down by sin and sickness and death, and God's love was so great, so indomitable, that God had to enter our world to join us and lead us. The kind of love that led God down from the majesty of heaven to a manger in tiny Bethlehem, and eventually, to a cross on a rocky hill outside Jerusalem. 'Love all lovely,' to quote Christina Rossetti, 'love incarnate, love divine.' Which is why "Emmanuel" is more than sweet sentiment or a pretty word that sounds lovely in carols; it's everything we believe Christmas to be about. God's love no longer offered from afar, but right up close. God no longer watching us from a distance. God actually *with us*.

"Frankly, if you ask me, it's the most important word in the Bible. *With*. Now, I know some of you are out there right now, scratching your head. Did he just say "with" is the most important word in the Bible? More important than love, or sin, or grace, or *God*? Well, yes, I did, because all those words are important and profound, and it's hard to imagine our faith without them, but for me, unless you have "with," everything else falls away. Until there is "with," there is no Emmanuel, no God with us, nor any of the things that the God-with-us accomplished.

"Not sure you agree? Think about this year. Among all the things we've lost this year (2020), the thing I think most of us have missed most has been the ability to be <u>with</u> each other. To love other people not from the safety of six-feet and behind a mask, but from the vulnerability and intimacy of close proximity. To lean in close, to put a hand on someone, to give them a hug. To be *with* them. Because there is a limit to loving people from a distance. There are some things Zoom just can't provide. Yes, among all the things we've learned this year, at the top is the lesson that being with each other means more than we ever knew.

"So maybe, as strange and hard as it is to celebrate a socially-distanced Christmas, maybe it's actually helping us better understand why God did it. Why God chose to leave the glories of heaven to come and live among us. Why God became a vulnerable human being like us, including that particularly beautiful vulnerability manifested in newborn babies. Because God knew, and God still knows, that actual physical presence means everything. Being with matters. To lean in close, to put a hand on someone, to give them a hug. Salvation was ultimately not something God could do from afar. God needed to be with us, just like Dan Grieb had to run that race *with* Chris Nikic. Because what God wanted to accomplish is only something you can do up close and personal. God knows that there's a limit to loving from a distance. So God came here, to love us up close, to be with us.

"That's why the story of the Nativity, of love coming down and dwelling among us, is not just a sweet bedtime story about something that happened long ago and far away. It is the perfect sign of who God is and how God will save us. Even in times like these. Even in a pandemic, even when fear and division and hatred crowd around us. God's answer to all our challenges remains the same today as on that first Christmas. Love that leads to sacrificial solidarity. Love that inspires costly companionship. Love that leads us to countless beautiful expressions of "with."

"Yes, a few weeks ago a young man became an Ironman. And he didn't do it alone. He had a companion, guide, and friend. Someone who was with him every step of the way.

"Tonight we remember how perfect Love became human, so that we don't have to do it alone. We have a companion, guide, and friend. His name is Jesus, but you can call him Emmanuel, because he is with us every step of the way. Amen." (by Rev. R. Casey Shobe)

CHAPTER FOURTEEN

Justin and Cynthia Walk

The group at the Kendrick house applauded the video with its clear-cut message. If Justin was embarrassed by his mother's lengthy "grandstanding," he kept his reaction to himself. Perhaps the isolation caused by Covid made everyone massively happy to be together, no matter what.

And then, there was a zoom call with family in Clarksdale, KS, which made Christmas perfect for the Florida Kendricks and their guests. Family gathered in Clarksdale were gathered indoors at the home of Julia and Marc, cozy with roaring fireplace, where on zoom, they met Christiane's soon to be new family. Family/familiarity, two words deeply meaningful during this Covid Christmas.

In Sandshell, James in his wheelchair was the first to leave the group, fatigued by the high-energy of so much social stimulation when he was accustomed to working in solitude in his home, long before others worked at home because of Covid.

After Justin walked James to his van and saw him off, Justin asked Cynthia if she'd care to walk around the block. His proposal massively thrilled and perplexed her at the same time. Through the years Justin had always been remote; friendly, decent, distant.

The two of them were scarcely on the sidewalk when he mentioned James going home alone. James, who often admitted he could have had a different life with Christiane and Jameson. Now seeming to live with endless regret.

Cynthia remembered Justin last Christmas, aware of James's needs at the beach. She also remembered Justin and Sherry last Christmas, meeting, dancing. There would be no dancing this Christmas because of Covid.

Cynthia, in a still-perplexed mood about why they were on a walk, observed, "Well, you go home alone, don't you, and is that so awful?" Justin wasn't dismayed by her pointed question, "Oh, no. I'd rather have my situation than to live with Monique. Is living with your parents awful? "Never awful," Cynthia qualified, "And being recently sick with bronchitis and taken care of with tender loving attention by my parents, I'd say it's a very good arrangement." Justin amazingly said, "Sherry told me you'd been ill, even in the hospital shortly."

"Antibiotics and loving care cured me," Cynthia summarized, while using his mention of Sherry to ask, "Are you and Sherry still together?" Justin needed to know, "What do you mean, together?" Cynthia attempted to clarify, "Dating, seeing each other, spending time together, romantically involved." He answered, "We mostly talk on the phone. Covid makes everything too complicated."

Cynthia didn't want her original question to die, "If there wasn't a pandemic, might you be planning on marrying Sherry? Justin dodged, "Hypotheticals are tricky, and reveal little that is substantial." Cynthia wouldn't let go, "Are you in love with Sherry." Justin laughed, "You really are like my mother!"

Cynthia was crushed, obvious by the look on her face as she looked at Justin square in the face. He put his arm around her momentarily, "That's not necessarily negative. Monique is remarkable. Like today, with the sermon she brought. She's gutsy, utterly dependable, has ridden out more storms than most people think about. She's forgiving—couldn't stand James after he left Christiane and Jameson—ended up helping him find a house here when she didn't want him moving here—has seen to it he gets one nutritious meal a day during the pandemic—includes him in holiday celebrations. Never talks bad about my dad, the divorce, his suicide. She's solid—a solid human being. I appreciate her more and more

while yet seeing her shortcomings, and not getting sucked into them."
They walked in silence.

Justin apologized, "I probably shouldn't have said you're like my
mother. Why do you think I asked you to go on this walk? I wanted to
have a conversation with you. We've known each other forever, and yet
never really talked—the two of us. Does one have to find love with someone new, or can there be love with someone well-known?

What was Justin saying?

He continued, "I've been infatuated, had crushes on you over the
years, but I was six years older, you were twelve years old when I was
eighteen; the age discrepancy was always too much. Then, I went away
to college. Then, you went away to college and graduate school while I
was here. I've always been intrigued with you but brushed it away, dis-
counted any possibility other than you as family friend.

"I remember how gutsy you were with Charles, he was older, bigger,
yet you had no fear confronting him."

Cynthia interrupted, "Actually, fear is why I so readily confronted
him, and it was Monique who told me powerlessness may have been un-
derlying my confrontational behavior, trying to embarrass Charles about
his obvious crush on Christiane who was too old for him. I was angry at
Monique for a long time, until I slowly realized she was correct in her
comment about my feeling powerless."

Justin changed the subject, "Francine promotes the idea that romantic attraction is not about love, but about attraction, physical attraction
and psychological attraction. Only now am I old enough, been through
enough relationships to understand what she was saying about the difference between love and attraction. I find Sherry very attractive, I'm attracted to her, partly because of her physical flair, partly because she is a
therapist, and I've needed a therapist. She's made it clear she can't be my
therapist, which makes complete sense. I agree.

"But you I like down deep. Maybe it is because you have traits like
Monique, qualities familiar to me, which echo inside me. This spur-of-
the-moment mention of going on a walk, I hadn't planned. Yet, I followed an impulse, and when you asked about Sherry and me, I became
honest, thoroughly transparent. I know there's this teacher Quinn in your
life, as Sherry has told me."

Cynthia felt light-headed. She'd need to sift through this, "My head is swimming. I need to make sense of what you've said. I often was en-amored with you but having tortured Charles about Christiane, I dare not let anyone know. Our families have just known each other for so long."

They walked in a cocoon of silence. Not awkward quiet, but a kind of vacuum. Yes, as if the air had been sucked out of the situation. Cynthia was afraid she might say something ghastly stupid. And she did.

" I find it strange that Charles married Dee's friend's daughter. Then, if you and I became a couple, again it would be Dee's friend's son. What's that about? Monique did mention you might be gay. How does that fit into all this?" Cynthia had blurted this against her intention to be sensible, reasonable. She wanted to run, physically run away from the conversa-tion, from Justin.

They came to the park Cynthia, Quinn, Bios and Pixie-Pickett fre-quented, which she explained to Justin. That again brought Quinn into the picture, which she hadn't intended. Horror grabbed her. However, Justin seemed not to notice and suggested they sit at a table.

Seated at a table across from each other, with Covid-prevention masks on, Justin threw back his head, and after a long skyward glance said, "The idea of me being gay was a stupid strategy of mine. Monique was forever bugging me about getting married, having children, giving her grandchildren, and I told her I might be gay to quiet her yammering. I should have known she'd tell others. That's all there is to that."

"What? I don't understand. That doesn't make sense." Cynthia would be her spontaneous self. She had this irrepressible side that would have its way, and at this moment she was grateful for it. She needed an expla-nation.

Justin was clear, "I've long known my mom's greatest fear is that I will be an economic failure, unable to earn a living. Her obsession about my dating stems from that fear, trying to lessen that fear, fixated with who I might marry, whether that someone could earn a living, as Monique largely had to do until my dad found his way, which took years.

"To get my mom off my back, I said to her, 'How do you know I'm not gay.' Something like that. I should have known she'd tell others, and in her imprecise way of speaking, who knows what she'd really say. But she did stop bugging me about marriage and grandchildren. Monique's fairly predictable while seeming hopelessly unpredictable."

Cynthia spoke uneasily, "I'm like that."

Justin admitted, "Maybe that's part of my attraction to you."

CHAPTER FIFTEEN

Justin Thinking Out Loud

Cynthia's thoughts were going haywire. She was immediately aware she would likely live her whole life in Florida if she bonded with Justin, and she so wanted to travel. She could become Cynthia Ammour, taking Justin's last name which looked French but was Algerian, or remain Cynthia Kendrick, or become Cynthia Ammour-Kendrick, or Kendrick-Ammour. Too much was going on in her head.

Should Cynthia and Justin become engaged, or whatever, perhaps married, which Cynthia couldn't really think about, Cynthia would have won-out over Sherry's glamour, which amused her. It was clear to Cynthia that Sherry mentioning Quinn had been the catalyst that caused Justin to reveal himself this Christmas Day to Cynthia, which was an overwhelming assumption on Cynthia's part. Was Justin jealous of Quinn? And what did that matter? Cynthia was trapped in her own world of suppositions, deductions, conclusions, speculations, questions.

Justin ended the silence, "You've probably heard Monique use the phrase she often uses with me and Christiane, 'Sit with it' meaning for us to reflect, ponder, turn something around in our minds to see if we've learned what we could from a situation or an idea, or what more we might consider.

"Yet Monique herself cannot long sit with anything. It's true, she has a quick mind, an alert nature; she is a fast learner, but she also is a selective learner. In her present love affair with the paintings of Marc Chagall, she has a small book given to her from the woman in whose home Monique first became infatuated with Chagall's paintings.

"Monique has shown me the small paperback, which the first owner carefully underlined and Monique lightheartedly, shrewdly told me, "From the first sentence I know the book is not for me even should I read it a hundred times; it is too dense for my understanding. But I have the gist of what its author says in what is underlined about what paintings bring to life; how paintings make the invisible visible. In my friend's underlinings I learn what I need to know on how paintings make the invisible world visible. And this I will one day share with the Brunch Bunch when I show them more Chagall paintings. His paintings I so love."

And then, Justin seemed to be thinking out loud, "I know what divorce does to a family and how devastating suicide is to those left to mourn. My dad's family was not religious. Coming from Algeria, one would expect them to be Muslim, yet they had no religion. I don't know the story behind that. I've asked Monique and she doesn't know either.

"I believe my dad had nothing to hold onto, to help him navigate life's difficulties. My mother's Catholicism was her rock-bottom strength. I see that more clearly the older I get. I also appreciate the aftermath of divorce in the life of Jameson who is shuttled back and forth between his parents. At least Christiane and I had one household to grow-up in, and there was solidarity and predictability in that.

"I am against divorce, because it brings continuing pain. It's easy to get married but maybe not to stay married. Passionate romance isn't the answer. Attraction, physically and psychologically, is important, but raw romance by itself has something false going on.

"I always knew I wasn't gay, however after using that crazy comment on my mother to get her off my back, I tried to imagine homosexual feelings, attractions. I sat with the possibility for a while. And when Monique spoke of my gayness, I got to experience my responses. It wasn't a planned experiment, but it turned out to be an informative experience that made me know homosexuality is not my inclination. Absolutely not.

"Initially, I did want Sherry for a therapist. I was attracted to her at first glance last Christmas. But then, all kinds of cautionary emotions kicked in: the unhealed strangeness of my parents' relationship; my mother's fears about me being like my father; realizing Sherry shouldn't be my therapist no matter how highly Francine regarded her. Sherry herself was adamant about not being my therapist.

"And then in March came Covid, and nothing was normal, especially not commercial real estate or being able to pursue a relationship with anyone while social distancing, mask wearing, and such abnormalities."

Cynthia listened while recalling feelings toward Justin when last Christmas Justin and Sherry danced through the kitchen and later when Sherry said he asked for her telephone number. Cynthia remembered feeling upset, sadness, regretful yearning when Sherry described Justin's arm around her shoulder meeting their first evening at the restaurant and the perfunctory hug that ended that evening. When Sherry, trying to assess her relationship with Justin told Cynthia of the embrace of their hands on the small balcony table the night of sharing Francine's folders, and the tame hug that ended that evening, which sent a ripple of tender hurt through Cynthia.

Sherry had concluded Justin wanted certainty more than romance in a relationship. He spoke as if exploring what he was looking for beyond romance. Sherry said he explained, "I remember growing up, in religion classes at church, talk about matrimony as a sacrament. I didn't understand most of what was being presented, but apparently the idea stuck with me. I need to go back and review what a sacrament is. I remember there were seven sacraments. But mostly, I remember that marriage was dealt with in some kind of sacred sense, as a means of grace, as something holy. I can likely find something about this online. The idea of marriage having a divine aura about it apparently appealed to me.

"Dating, I've learned relationships aren't simple or easy; they can be satisfying as well as heartbreaking. But if two people marry with the shared idea that their life together can be an avenue of religious significance, spiritual satisfaction, then that might strengthen the relationship."

"Jameson will soon live with a new father and two new sisters who will stay sometimes at his house, while Jameson will continue to visit his own father. Divorce, if children are involved, brings continuing pain. I repeat, it seems easy to get married but maybe not to stay married. Maybe no one *gets* married, but has to *become* married. Passionate romance isn't the answer. I always knew I wasn't gay, and should never have done that to Monique, but she can be more than annoying, and sometimes needs to be stopped. That was cruel of me." Justin became quiet.

CHAPTER SIXTEEN

Cynthia and That Oral Conversation

They remained seated at the table in the park. Birds could be heard, a few distant sounds, everything seemed peaceful and lovely. This Christmas day was becoming coolish as the sun *lowered* in the sky; Cynthia was grateful to put on the sweater she'd tied around her waist. She didn't know what to do with all Justin had just shared. She had always been attracted to him, but never given that a second thought because of the age difference, and in her mind, he was simply part of Monique's family, a *family* friend.

She decided to make light of the heavy ideas flooding her mind, "Yes, I'll need to sit with all you've said. Do you find it strange that the sermon your mother read today also emphasized the word *with*, though in a different context than to *sit with*."

Justin agreed, "Now that you make the connection, yes. Just like I find it strange I shared what I did *with you*, the most unlikely, yet the only person it makes sense I might have shared with. I could have kept quiet and lived with the consequences. Instead, I spilled deepest feelings and will live with the consequences. Silence isn't always golden. Sometimes it makes the most sense to go out on a limb, reveal oneself, and see what happens."

Cynthia decided to reveal herself, "What if I don't remember correctly what you've said today. What if I don't correctly interpret what I think you said? An oral conversation is imprecise, words disappearing the moment they are spoken, compared to a written statement, yet that's not quite true, for a written statement does not convey voice tone, body language, though the words remain permanently on the paper and one can re-read them endlessly. A conversation is tied to sound, whereas a written statement is visual.

"In graduate school I read a book that talked about human awareness, consciousness, how all understanding changes when reading and writing enter culture, compared to a strictly or mostly oral culture. Only now, today, this moment do I experience the importance of that book, now when I am questioning whether my memory will serve me well in this instance."

Justin boldly summarized, "I've suggested we consider whether we can be life-partners, companions, lovers, parents, staying with each other through thick and thin. Married."

A shiver went through Cynthia, which Justin noticed and suggested, "Perhaps we should go back, it is getting cooler." There beside the park table was a spontaneous lengthy embrace between two masked people, which must have been amusing should anyone be watching. Cynthia burying her head on his shoulder, the power of touch most extraordinary. He added, knowing he was repeating, "Can long-time family friends get married? Must one always marry a stranger?"

They walked arm-in-arm until near the Kendrick house. Cynthia had to explain to herself and to Justin, "You knew ahead of time what you were going to say, so the words you said today were familiar to you. Everything you said to me was new to me; I hadn't an inkling. I may not have absorbed your whole line of thought. I'm still trying to put it all together."

They became quiet, walking. Inside herself, Cynthia feverishly understood clearly for the first time that the New Zealand teacher, Sylvia Ashton Warner who developed her own reading tactics with native Maori children was dealing with the oral mindset of Maori students contrasted with the children who came from homes where reading and writing were prevalent.

A whole new chapter opened in Cynthia's brain. She loved teaching children to read and write, though this unpredictable Covid-year had been truly taxing. She was grateful Quinn helped her through some tough teaching hurdles. Yes, there was Quinn in her life.

Cynthia and Justin were now on the Kendrick block, no longer walking arm-in-arm, and then entered the Kendrick backyard where Zach was about to light the firepit, where sandwiches and finger foods would be brought to the patio table, and later, Christmas carols sung as everyone was seated round the pit, flames dancing, a hypnotic aura alive this night; this truly unusual night.

The long absence of Justin and Cynthia that afternoon was not lost on the adults, though no one commented, not even Monique.

It took Cynthia a long time to fell asleep that night remembering what Justin said about consequences, 'I could have kept quiet and lived with the consequences. Instead, I spilled deepest feelings and will live with the consequences. Silence isn't always golden. Sometimes it makes the most sense to go out on a limb, reveal oneself, and see what happens.'

Cynthia awakened the day after Christmas, Saturday, with "consequences" on her mind. She recalled Sherry talking about there being no devil or Satan, only consequences. Collective consequences of good or bad choices, stemming from the innate opposites of all possibility, all potentiality, as if humans need to take responsibility for their own choices, decisions, actions, and not blame outside sources. Was Justin influenced by Sherry's emphasis on consequences? Cynthia would need to ask him. She still felt unsure about the place of Sherry in Justin's life.

Cynthia remembered Dee had emphasized consequences in her explication of the parables. Cynthia felt hesitant about asking Justin anything, remembering he'd said she was like Monique. Would she be able to live with that? Being labeled as similar to his mother . . .

Cynthia lay in bed upon awakening that Saturday morning after Christmas. There would be another week without school, heading into New Year's Eve, New Year's Day, 2021, a new year; the old year 2020 having been difficult with Covid, and Reggie, Estelle's husband, dying.

But then, 2020 had been strangely OK, too. Cynthia found a job in Sandshell, begotten Pixie-Pickett, met Quinn—and having a marriage proposal from Justin? She was amused, perplexed, overwhelmed, having to deal with too much at this moment, and knowing herself pretty well, she knew she'd need someone to talk *with* about all of this. She could 'sit *with* it' but she'd do better if someone else was sitting *with* her, at least part of the time, and listening to her, talking *with* her. It couldn't be Sherry.

She wondered if it might have been better had Justin simply asked her out for an evening. Perhaps he felt under pressure because of Quinn. Cynthia wanted to laugh and keep laughing that she was a much-coveted woman—two males pursuing her? However, Quinn had never indicated she was his choice for sharing a Greek Island in the summer. Yet, he was thoughtful, meeting her and Pixie-Pickett and going to the park; the same park now indelibly imprinted with Justin's marriage proposal.

Cynthia remained in bed, thinking again of all that Justin said and how the words disappeared in the air, not written-down anywhere, with no *evidence*—perhaps only her mind imagined, manufactured aspects or implications of the conversation. Or, she could get up, have breakfast, and then decide what she'd do next; how she'd deal with what she assumed was accurate memory of a conversation that took place yesterday with Justin.

Never before had she appreciated how fragile oral conversation is, yet how powerful the impact it carries even when not written down. But everything seems written down these days, or recorded, or videoed. As the book she read in graduate school indicated, consciousness is bound to shift when culture shifts from oral to alphabet literacy which took centuries of change. Then more centuries and handwriting became mechanized with the printing press, linotype, typewriters, word processors, and then another technological shift to a kind of second-orality that has widespread pictures, images on television, electronic devices, face-timing each other, zoom calls, police cams.

Was Cynthia's brain thinking theoretical things to escape what was too much, too immense for her to handle? Just then, she remembered Sherry saying it seemed Justin wanted certainty more than romance in a relationship. That was it! Cynthia had a breakthrough. Justin was ready to get married, and wanted someone safe to marry. She, Cynthia, was that safe someone!

She threw back covers, sprang from her bed, put on robe and slippers, walked with Pixie-Pickett into the kitchen where Zach and Dee were lingering at the breakfast table, talking. They had just ended a conversation about the Cynthia-Justin walk yesterday and were onto another topic before Cynthia and Pickett entered the room.

Dad-Zach asked, "Sleep well?" Cynthia replied, "Maybe. I can't be sure. I'm so glad you're both here, as I need you to sit with me a bit," and she told them her story of the potential marriage proposal, as she had coffee and breakfast. Never, never, would they have guessed the story she told was the reason for yesterday's walk. And yet . . .

CHAPTER SEVENTEEN

Justin Ruminating Alone

That same morning, in the neighboring beach town of Fort Hayden, Justin was reflecting in his apartment on what he'd proposed to Cynthia yesterday. He hadn't planned to be that explicit. It seemed the pressure of the moment had him saying more than he meant to say. But then, maybe it was better that way—play with the biggest ball possible and see what happens. At least it will generate an interesting response, or maybe a deadening one, depending on Cynthia's response.

Justin found clear-cut parameters easier to deal with than blurred-edges. He preferred high stakes. He hadn't tried to mislead, frighten or confuse Cynthia. He might have done all three. It was true, he'd always liked her, but he was in college when she was not yet in high school. The thought of expressing feelings about Cynthia never crossed his mind until Sherry mentioned Quinn.

He wondered what their spontaneous hug yesterday meant? Perhaps she was embarrassed with his forthrightness, overcome with such talk, nearly faint from shock? He speculated. He thought his line about consequences was brilliant. He'd be damned if he didn't propose to her and she married Quinn, or he'd be damned if he did propose and she said, "no." Is that how that went? It seemed so clear when he first said it. Now he wasn't sure of the exact words he used yesterday.

He knew what she meant when she said words not written down, evaporate in the air. Should he have written a script, read it aloud to her, given her a copy and kept the original for himself, or something like that. That would have been weird. He knew plenty about contracts and preliminary contracts at work. What he proposed with Cynthia wasn't a business arrangement.

Why did he now, just now, get entangled with marriage and the thought of Cynthia? It was true, he recently made a lot of money, was feeling confident in commercial real estate. He'd also learned something with Covid, the importance of living near family, not living a thousand miles away, or across the Atlantic Ocean like Monique and Henri left their families in France.

He'd been on fire to connect with Cynthia after Sherry told him about Quinn and Cynthia. Justin had come to know he was not permanently connected with Sherry, though he found her glamorous, exceptionally bright and interesting. There was something about Cynthia. Maybe because she was like his mother. He wanted to pursue that more with the male therapist in Fort Hayden he'd been seeing. He knew Cynthia wasn't Catholic, but Dee was, so Cynthia knew some about Catholicism.

He preferred marrying someone who had a religious base to draw from, like Monique was able to get from Catholicism. He knew he'd have to seek, find, discern religious stuff himself, as he felt his dad didn't have a foundation like that which could help sustain him. Justin also thought religion could be goofy, radical, fanatical and he had no use for that. The Catholic Church has its own messes to clean up with the priest pedophile scandals, and declining church attendance.

Dee was a sensibly religious person. He did not like when Cynthia was sharp with Dee, as he'd seen in the past. Cynthia had had to grow-up. There was a lot he and Cynthia would have to discuss. They'd never really talked over the years. Not really. To have known each other so long and so little was almost an accomplishment of some sort. Charles was a good sort, and so was Zach. Does one have to marry a stranger instead of marry someone known to them, and to know their family as well? He kept asking this question.

Of course, Justin didn't know how Cynthia felt about him. He rather agreed with Francine's skeptical view of romantic love. He'd been through the 'love' thing. He agreed 'liking' someone is more important. He'd liked Cynthia for years—intermittently, depending on what was going on romantically in his life, and when he'd seen her again over a holiday. It was a special 'like' he had for Cynthia.

Covid probably helped Justin not become involved with Sherry. It was better that way. There was something about Cynthia, her snippy little face and personality. He felt real concern when Sherry said Cynthia was struggling with teaching online. He wondered from spending time with Jameson, how anybody could teach second graders partly online, especially a first-time teacher? And then this guy Quinn was being thoughtful and supportive, Sherry said. At a time of vulnerability, one can be very emotionally vulnerable, Justin concluded.

Sherry had met Quinn at Kendricks on Thanksgiving and spoke well of him to Justin who began planning to move Quinn out of Cynthia's life if that was possible, upon hearing from Sherry she would be with her family in Georgia for Christmas while Quinn would be with a coach from the high school and his family.

Justin hadn't asked Sherry whether the relationship between Cynthia and Quinn seemed serious, for Sherry was a psychotherapist, and therapists pick up on everything, and he did not want Sherry to suspicion his interest in Cynthia.

The walk yesterday seemed to have a life of its own. His original plan was to suggest the two of them going out sometime. They had rarely spoken at holidays over the years when he and Charles, as well as he and Zach conversed more. He'd probably always been self-conscious around Cynthia, too enamored of her to be relaxed. Would Cynthia believe such nonsense? Or did Monique dominate the holidays with the Kendricks, leaving Justin barely noticed?

He returned to the evaporation of spoken words, knowing also that words might be gone but not forgotten. It was too late to take yesterday's words back. A situation now existed, and he was rather OK with the prospect of a jolting situation at hand. Go for broke, he told himself. All or nothing suited him. The words needed to be said yesterday.

CHAPTER EIGHTEEN

Sharing with Dad – Zach and Mum-Dee

While Justin was conversing with himself this Saturday morning, in the Kendrick kitchen Cynthia told Dee and Zach everything about yesterday's walk. Neither seemed taken-aback, surprised, or shocked. However, Zach started laughing . . . and laughing. Cynthia was perplexed, and so was Dee.

"Dad, this isn't funny. It's not a joke. Justin was serious, and I'm telling this as it happened. It's not meant to be amusing."

"I know, I know . . . it's real . . . I can't stop . . . it's really funny . . . but it's not funny at all." He tried to straighten himself, but peals of laughter continued. The females looked at each other. He'd had a panic-attack years ago, was this a laugh-attack?

Cynthia got up and poured herself another cup of coffee, while Zach was trying to get himself sober. Having restrained himself, he began to explain, "It's just that for years I've asked myself why the two of you weren't attracted to each other. I kept thinking, 'There's something there' and yet there wasn't. The next holiday would come and go, I'd have the same impression, but there was no response, no indication, no hint on the part of the two actors—no one acting out the roles I had going on in my head.

"I decided there was something weird about me. Yesterday when you went on a walk, I had the same inkling that there was a special bond between the two of you. Talk about women's intuition! I must have an abundance of it. Was it wishful thinking on my part? Projection? Perhaps Monique and family have been so like family some part of me turned the situation into actual family. I was an only child, you know."

"But why is that funny, " Cynthia inquired, "I don't understand."

"You'd have to be inside my head to understand. It's funny only because I've known this connection existed as clear as anything long before it came to pass. I was sure inside myself."

"But what if I'm not interested in Justin's point of view, his perspective, his proposal. Then you'd be wrong."

"I'd be wrong concerning you but not him."

Cynthia needed to know more precisely, "You're not laughing out of pure joy that this has come to pass for me? That Justin is pursuing me in reaction to Quinn? "

"I don't know. I'd say the humor is simply that for a long time I've known something like this would happen. Maybe it's not humor, maybe more like a witch's cackle inside me."

"You think it's weird," Cynthia pressed.

"I don't think it's weird. I think I'm weird. Don't be offended. When I pursued the topic of marriage with Dee, I remember saying something about being willing to make a fool of myself feeling I wanted to be with her permanently, trying to get her to move back here from Connecticut, so we could get to know each other better. On one hand, I was a fool to be so transparent to her. On the other hand, I was mature enough to share my feelings, to risk."

Cynthia pressed further, "And did you think he was weird, Dee, for saying that?"

"Not weird. No, not weird. I wanted to be with him and was grateful he risked letting me know his feelings. Otherwise, I would perhaps have stayed in Connecticut and languished. Who knows how these things work."

Dee elaborated, "Synchronistically, his stark proposal came as I'd just uncovered some metaphoric insights about myself with Ann Dramm. I was living with newfound independence, and thus able to announce on the spot that I wanted to return to Florida, and to Zach, though I didn't say the part including Zach. However, Zach said, 'Then why don't you simply come back' and I said I was going to do just that. It was all fairly simple. Of course, I was nearly twenty years older than you are now, for whatever difference that might make."

Cynthia wanted more personal information from her dad, "What about when you and Roxanne decided to marry. Who asked whom?"

"We were seniors in college. I'm not sure there was ever an official proposal by anybody. At some point we just knew we were a couple and would one day marry, which we did as soon as we graduated."

Cynthia was overwhelmed, clearly overwhelmed. She needed to talk with Charles, but today was Saturday, he was likely at work at the furniture store.

CHAPTER NINETEEN

At the Beach

That afternoon Justin picked-up Cynthia after a morning phone call from him in which they made afternoon plans to go to a stretch of beach other than Fort Hayden or Sandshell. He brought two beach chairs with attached umbrellas, drinks packed in ice, and they stopped to buy snacks. How do you create a scene adequate to talking about the rest of your life? Where does one go to find answers to life-changing questions?

Justin had had time to think about what Cynthia was just now thinking. She realized Sherry met Quinn Thanksgiving at the Kendricks, mentioned Quinn to Justin, and thus Justin's reaction began several weeks ago. However, Cynthia learned only yesterday, Christmas, what was churning inside Justin. She had little time to ponder, cogitate, ruminate, acclimate. What should have been, might have been, could have been a joyful time for Cynthia, felt ominous, too big, worrisome and heavy to her.

Justin knew not to push Cynthia. Monique often tried to push Justin, which is what led him to make the knee-jerk statement, "I might be gay," as Monique tried to force him into a committed relationship. He said one thing, but she understood another. In his mind he was saying, 'For all you know, I might be gay,' to deflect, spoil, set-aside, overturn her ambitious plans for him, derail her determined effort that he fulfill her agenda on her timetable. However, Monique interpreted his comment not as a hypothetical but as a fact, 'I might be gay.'

Justin wondered what words of his yesterday on Christmas might have meant one thing to him and something else to Cynthia. What is said isn't always what is received. Justin hadn't read Dee's fourfold explication of Jesus' parables, but he'd seen Sherry's copy of Dee's work. He saw what Dee did with the parables, and the idea of the fourfold format made sense to Justin. He appreciated complexity; many angles, viewpoints of buyers and sellers, finances, financial institutions in commercial real estate.

As the afternoon at the beach progressed, Cynthia found Justin a good listener who understood hermeneutics because of the pipeline between Dee and The Brunch Bunch. Reading-specialist Cynthia was again talking about the difference between a mostly oral personality and a heavily engaged reading-writing personality.

"The more an adult personality is a reading and writing personality, the more the personality can re-read material, analyze an idea or concept. Therefore, a highly literate (reading-writing) personality is prone to be more analytical than a mostly oral personality.

"When I think about what you said yesterday, I remember approximately, not exactly. However, if you'd recorded as you spoke to me, then I could listen to the recording and re-hear what you said repeatedly, and if I want to, use an alphabet and write each word. I'd say we seldom think of how modes of communication, oral, writing, reading, listening, seeing, change culture, change human consciousness.

"With radio we hear only, with TV we see and hear, and now texting, we digitize, transmit and receive. Everything impacts our consciousness. My young online students have a different consciousness than I had at their age because of their electronic gadgets, learning online.

"Dee has journals and journals of her dreams. She takes dreams, which are mostly pictures, writes them into words, and the mere process of putting them into words she feels has transformed her through the years. Sometimes she sketches dreams which has its own impact on consciousness.

"I wonder whether today's social-media shows us that the general populace has only pragmatic, shallow, superficial knowledge about themselves which flows back and forth, hither and yon, and whether this means too many of us are unacquainted with roots of our own fears, angers, powerlessness. I have deduced this from Francine and from Dee's humanities professor friend, Oriana.

"From Dee I've learned Christianity is not merely or mostly a moral code, a way to live, to act and behave, but more importantly a re-orientation in the cosmos, especially with oneself, a journey of self-knowledge, which forms a seedbed of wisdom to live well, to live with integrity. Christianity is about transformation of the personality into its potential by aligning one's life with divine intention, thus contributing to the common good. Only very recently did I figure this out, and I'd say to a large extent from Quinn who was in a seminary for a short time where he learned being a priest wasn't for him."

Justin immediately responded, "And what about Quinn?"

"Quinn is a person of real substance, well read, well informed. Spent time in the army, two tours of military duty in Afghanistan, has a sense of humor. He's dependable. A well-regarded teacher at Merriweather."

"Are you in love with him?"

"Influenced by Francine's sober view of *in-loveness* I don't really talk about such."

Shocked, Justin reminded, "Yesterday you asked me if I am in love with Sherry."

"I did? Yes, I guess I did, and you said I'm like your mother. No wonder I repressed that specific verbal exchange. Quinn and I have not talked about the future. That might be because of Covid. We've never known each other in normal times. He's certainly understood my teaching struggle and going to the park daily with the dogs has helped me stay sane."

"He can talk about lots of things. When I talked to him about a shift in human consciousness with the change from only oral communication to the alphabet and writing, then to printing with the printing press, and now to electronic ways of communicating he was able to add something about Jesus being called the Word made Flesh, and the bible being labeled the Word of God."

Justin was not overly-impressed, "Having attended a seminary it's reasonable to assume he'd know things like that." And then added, "Has he ever watched Bishop Barron or the Franciscan priest Richard Rohr, international author, on YouTube? I've recently discovered them on YouTube and find them profound. I'm not wanting to compete with Quinn, just trying to understand your relationship with him."

Cynthia blinked, thinking, only saying, "I'd say Quinn and I are friends. Period." However, Cynthia realized she felt threatened by Quinn's possible attraction to Sherry on Thanksgiving. But then, Cynthia always felt second to Sherry when it came to style, physical appeal. She would use this opportunity to get Justin's perspective on Sherry's attractiveness.

CHAPTER TWENTY

Fate or Destiny

Cynthia pushed her inquiry, "On Thanksgiving, Quinn and Sherry met for the first time and I felt sure Quinn would be entranced by Sherry as you were last Christmas when you met her."

"How do you know I was entranced by her?"

"You danced with her through the kitchen, then you contacted her, the two of you were together before Covid came, and you've stayed in touch even until now."

"Didn't know you were keeping track."

"Sherry and I share," Cynthia laughed at the redundancy.

"Did she indicate we have a serious relationship; that we've talked about a future together?

"No."

"Hmmm . . . If you and Quinn are friends, can't Sherry and I be friends?"

"Don't be condescending."

"I'm trying to explore our present situation, which I can't do unless we talk—each of us be as real as can be."

"I feel scared right now," Cynthia ventured.

"I don't mean to be condescending. Maybe I also have feelings of stress and uncertainty."

Cynthia remembered the morning conversation with Zach and Dee, when Zach told how talking by telephone to Dee in Stamford, CT he was willing to make a fool of himself letting her know he wanted to be with her permanently, trying to get her to move back to Sandshell from Stamford. Zach said on one hand, he was a fool to be so transparent, but on the other hand, he was mature enough to risk sharing his feelings with her. Dee said she was, indeed, most grateful he let her know his feelings. Cynthia shared this with Justin who responded.

"What you just told about your parents makes me feel OK with what I started yesterday with you, though I've had weeks and the sounding board of a therapist to think about this while you've had one day. Since it concerns the rest of our lives, we needn't rush."

Impulsively, Cynthia bent sideways, playfully kissed his hairy arm resting on the armrest of his chair, and immediately felt stupid for doing so, her seated body bent forward, head somewhat down. Why had she done that? Yes, she'd liked what he said about having the rest of their lives.

Justin put his hand on her shoulder which felt beautiful, strong, tender, reassuring. Her long secret attraction to Justin was reciprocated, actively received by him. Cynthia reflected that for someone like herself, prone to say whatever came to mind, she had never mentioned her feelings for him to anyone, not anyone.

Just now, she veered away from feelings and inserted a social comment, "With today's electronic communications, brief toxic wording can convey lethal messages to masses of people who feel they are 'in the know' because of highly-charged, simplistic, emotional snippets. She told herself, *I believe messages of grievance and fear appeal to people with little background in broad-based humanities, or in knowing themselves.* Cynthia realized she was, in ways, repeating herself, and knew also that she was not a systematic thinker.

Her mind flipped to wondering about humans these days endlessly thinking, processing, cogitating, ruminating about themselves. She remembered the book in graduate school on orality and literacy, on the how an oral culture does not deal in articulated self-analysis. The author of that book mentioned growing literacy and the evolution of consciousness, the growing awareness of self in the depths of the psyche.

Cynthia thought about Dee and hermeneutics, the purple aura of the cat, interpreting herself psychologically through metaphoric discernment. In today's electronically-connected world, can we know when we are being manipulated? What did 'Know Thyself' of Greek Delphi mean? Was Justin meeting with a psychotherapist so as to realize, actualize, to know himself more completely, and therein he discovered his longtime deep feelings for Cynthia? Was he uncovering his fate, destiny? Did his fate or destiny mesh with Cynthia's fate or destiny? She asked him this question.

He said he didn't know much about fate or destiny, but asked if she had ever seen the 2001 movie, *Serendipity*, "It's a predictable story, maybe schmaltzy, and doesn't parallel our situation because a couple falls in love at their first chance meeting which starts everything between them, whereas we've known each other for forever. I watched the movie with Christiane after her divorce and she said she didn't believe in fate or destiny at that time. Now that she's met Carter, I need to ask what she believes along those lines."

Cynthia hadn't seen the movie, so after the beach they went to Justin's condo, watched the movie, and then tried to figure out whether fate and destiny are specific and narrow or more general and broad-based, whether humans have any input in the decision, or if fate or destiny even exist.

CHAPTER TWENTY-ONE

Two Couples Revealed

Driving to Justin's condo, Cynthia found she was more interested in seeing his condo than watching the movie. In the condo she observed indications of home decorating flair, but mostly it was plain vanilla, utilitarian, reasonably neat. And strange above all, after the movie they ate food left from the Kendrick Christmas feast yesterday, he'd brought to his apartment, which was hilarious to both of them; epitomizing their relationship. "There's something almost incestuous about how closely our families are connected," Cynthia observed.

One character in the movie *Serendipity* said, "If we are to live life in harmony with the universe, we must all possess a powerful faith in what the ancients used to call *fatum,* what we currently refer to as destiny." Cynthia questioned the idea, "Seems to me discernment is necessary or one can end up trusting in silly stuff." Then she affirmed the idea, "Seems like synchronicity does happen."

Justin added, "Monique watched the movie with Christiane and me and she afterwards commented, 'See what fruit certain people or situations bring. Judge by the fruit. Since Henri's divorce and suicide, I'm not sure in fate, destiny, or anything such. Maybe we have only moments, and how each moment seems to us. Humans are not well-capable to make decisions, yet we must."

And then Monique had second thoughts, "I don't believe in fate or destiny as put onto you. No, I don't believe in that, but in doing God's will, which is not put on you but you uncover, discover for yourself through prayer, to do the will of God. That is different. It comes out from relationship between you and God."

As Cynthia and Justin talked, he mentioned a Bishop Robert Barron video on YouTube on the topic of 'Your Life is not About You.' Justin and Cynthia watched the short video. To Cynthia, being with Justin felt right and comfortable, thrilling and fulfilling. Was that enough to make a marriage?

The next day, Sunday, Justin had a work engagement, which rarely took place on Sunday, but nothing was normal during Covid. And then he'd be back to work on Monday, whereas Cynthia had more days off before she'd be back dealing with students and teaching strategies. She wanted to be *with* students, as the sermon Monique brought on Christmas, emphasized.

Cynthia was thinking about Quinn, Sherry, New Year's Eve in a few days. Could she handle Monique as a mother-in-law? Justin mentioned Bishop Barron twice, likely planning on becoming a practicing Catholic again, she assumed, and how would that work if they married? They needed a lengthy discussion about this.

Dee hadn't inflicted her religion practice on Charles and Cynthia. But then, Charles became a Catholic anyway after he met chanting monks in a movie, and his beloved Kendal. His fate was sealed. Cynthia didn't disagree with Bishop Barron on the video, but she'd need to watch the video again. She knew her dad's negative view of Church hierarchy, some of Church history. She'd need to watch more Bishop Barron videos to gauge her reaction to the bishop and his ideas.

Justin was busy the week between Christmas and New Year's Eve. He spoke with Cynthia every evening. In the afternoon, she and Pixie-Pickett went to the park with Quinn and Bios. Sherry was back in town, engaging with clients in virtual therapy. She and Cynthia texted short messages. Sherry and Justin texted some.

A dam of human emotion was building inside Cynthia who calculated she was at the center of this unwieldly foursome, the person primarily connected to each of the other three, and therefore she needed to set things straight, bring everything out in the open. She continued to wonder what was everyone doing New Year's Eve?

It was Wednesday afternoon, the day before New Year's Eve, Quinn came by the Kendrick house for Cynthia and Pixie-Pickett, and the usual walk to the park. She felt she would burst if she didn't reveal a faint outline of her new relationship with Justin. But wouldn't it make more sense for her to first tell Sherry?

The sniffing dogs and their human counterparts walked to the park, the humans chatting about any number of unimportant matters. Then, seated on the same park bench where she and Justin had been Christmas Day, Cynthia blurted out, "On Christmas Day, a most amazing event took place at this very spot. Sitting here with Monique's son, Justin, whom I've known for years, we shared our mutual romantic interest in each other. Sherry and Justin have been dating or semi-dating since they met last Christmas. I have yet to share with Sherry what I've just told you."

Cynthia, overwrought, looked at Quinn, while he, with a smile on his face, looked out at the scenery, and then he looked at Cynthia, "Sherry and I, since meeting at your house on Thanksgiving have been keeping in touch, spending time together. We've been discussing how to tell you, for her to tell Justin."

Is that why Sherry told Justin about Quinn and Cynthia? Cynthia was confused, overcome at this convoluted sequence of events; couldn't make sense of any of the present dynamics. But she felt relieved. She had correctly surmised Quinn would be impressed upon meeting Sherry on Thanksgiving. Yet, actually, none of that mattered now. Cynthia was unburdened; everything was out in the open. Quinn would tell Sherry about Cynthia and Justin. Above all, Cynthia no longer felt sneaky.

Just then, Quinn said, "It feels good for everything to have come full circle, and hopefully we can all remain friends. Don't you think this is possible?"

"Yes, of course. That is what I want," agreed Cynthia, grateful Quinn stated her ardent desire. Cynthia realized how correct brother Charles had been when they finally got to discuss her newfound relationship with Justin, whom he knew almost like a brother, now as a prospective brother-in-law, which delighted Charles.

Charles met Sherry last Christmas, but having never met Quinn, Charles concluded, "Knowing three-fourths of the troupe involved, I suspect this will work-out well for you mature people. I love Justin, but you must not marry him just because he's proposed the idea, or because I am fond of him, as I know your own high regard for my opinions and affections," he facetiously informed her. Charles was light-hearted about this possible marriage between Cynthia and Justin.

Meanwhile, Justin was indeed busy at work. Having the recent large property transaction finalized, meant he was viewed in a new light by other realtors, which meant expectations of what he was capable increased. He didn't want to be swallowed by his job, yet he wanted to maximize opportunities for himself. He knew what it was like to live with high-powered realtor Monique, too often over-worked, stressed as wife and mother.

He was amused that evening hearing on the phone with Cynthia about the tell-all exchange between herself and Quinn in the park, and Justin remarked, "I felt a path would open, making everything clear for everybody. I'm sure Sherry and I will soon have the same conversation. The only person I'm not wanting to know anything about this is my mother, which seems best just now."

He suggested, "Our first priority is to plan New Year's Eve," which they agreed they'd spend together at Justin's place. How does a couple who's known each other for a long time, but was just now discovering each other, celebrate New Year's Eve during a pandemic? There were no public parties at country clubs, hotels, bars available. It would have been great to dress elegantly and dance-in the new year. Surely 2021 would be an improvement over 2020.

On New Year's Eve, long-acquainted Cynthia and Justin were together at Justin's condo, while recently-met Sherry and Quinn were together at Sherry's enchanted beach dwelling to bring in 2021, with hopes the new year would bring political calm and widespread vaccine to end the pandemic. The new year simply must be better than the old year had been.

CHAPTER TWENTY-TWO

Conscience

However, less than a week later, on January 6, 2021, the U.S. Capitol was stormed by protesters (quickly labeled 'domestic insurrectionists') vandalizing, threatening, forcing a joint session of Congress gathered to count electoral votes confirming President-elect Joseph R. Biden Jr.'s victory over President Donald J. Trump, to evacuate the House Chamber and seek shelter from harm.

The volatile mob, focused on harming Vice President Mike Pence and Speaker of the House Nancy Pelosi, had been invited by Trump to Washington, D.C. on this date, still claiming the election in November had been stolen from him, despite evidence this was not true. Five died in the tumult of January 6, none of them legislators.

At the same time, Covid-19 numbers rose dramatically from holiday travel. Nationally, the new year had a turbulent beginning and this was true for Cynthia and Justin and for Sherry and Quinn as well. For the couples, not immediately in the new year, but eventually.

As the initial newness of their exclusive relationships became dependable and routine both couples began to realize heartfelt differences. Cynthia was more liberal in her social justice leanings than Justin who felt individuals need to take more responsibility for themselves. Sherry had come to prefer a sacramental brand of Christianity and felt inclined toward becoming Anglican Catholic (Episcopal) which ordains women deacons and priests rather than Roman Catholic which does not ordain women, while Quinn was committed to Roman Catholicism.

Sherry was now comprehending more profoundly the struggles of Kelly and Paul, the married couple continuing therapy, trying to work through their differences and improve their marriage. Quinn and Bios continued to run from their condo to the Kendrick residence to pick up Cynthia and Pixie-Pickett for a walk to the park and back. Cynthia and Quinn came to share somewhat with each other the political, religious points of contention with their significant-other. This had indeed worked-out in a strange way between these four people.

Cynthia was influenced by her father's views on affordable housing, and how some people need help improving their lot in life. She was shaped by Dee's spiritual sense that personal transformation is everyone's greatest need, and becoming a teacher herself, Cynthia realized learning is not a one-size-fits-all proposition. Some students simply need more help or a different kind of help for them to learn.

Whereas Justin was motivated by will-power, assuming responsibility, not making excuses, expecting much effort from everyone, which he learned from the sheer effort of his mother, and he had fear of an insipid response to what life demands, from reactions he saw in his father.

Justin was thoughtful and compassionate towards James, Christiane's ex, for James earned a good living, had a strong work ethic. Justin admitted his father Henri was easier to live with than Monique, though his mother was better at earning a living. Justin had lots of clashing promptings within his personality, which he was uncovering in therapy.

Sherry had at times entertained the possibility of one day becoming an ordained minister, following in her father's footsteps. She felt tying the personality to interpretations of scripture as Dee had done with Jesus' parables, can be profound, and she agreed that personality transformation is largely what the word 'salvation' alludes to; healing, making whole the personality, as in psychotherapy. She was thus considering joining the Episcopal Church, fully sacramental and ordaining women, rather than the Roman Catholic Church, sacramental, but with no ordination of women.

Quinn's family was many generations Roman Catholic. He didn't want a split-church marriage, spouses not attending church together, having children raised in such an arrangement. This was profoundly problematic to Quinn.

Together, Sherry and Quinn began looking for a solution to this problem. He read in a Vatican II document:

> Deep within their consciences men and women discover a law which they have not laid upon themselves and which they must obey. Its voice, ever calling them to love and to do what is good and to avoid evil, tells them inwardly at the right moment: do this, shun that. For they have in their hearts a law inscribed by God. Their dignity rests in observing this law, and by it they will be judged. The conscience is people's most secret core, and their sanctuary. There they are alone with God whose voice echoes in their depths.[2]

Quinn and Sherry talked about the voice of conscience. At one point Sherry noted, "The authors are describing psychologically healthy people, not sociopaths, sometimes referred to as psychopaths, who have little or no conscience. They also are not describing personalities with too much guilt or shame, some who've been brow-beaten by unhealthy religion, who sometimes come in for therapy.

"Sociopaths do not seek therapy. Most people pursue therapy to become more comfortable with themselves or their situation. Sociopaths lack the capacity to feel uncomfortable with themselves, and tend to go to prison having no guilt about what they've done. Sociopaths might be in politics, or in other powerful positions where they have no guilt or shame about stepping on others to get ahead. They tend to be exceptionally charming, have a knack for knowing what others want to hear, are excellent con-artists, scammers and schemers, and can be utterly ruthless, heartless."

---

[2] *The Basic Sixteen Documents, Vatican Council II*, general editor Austin Flannery, (1996), p. 178.

Quinn and Sherry realized they shared the basic Christian story. This wasn't an issue between them. Tradition was the problem; the ordination of women. And so, the two of them talked about conscience, following one's conscience. Conscience isn't a psychological term, but more a metaphysical concept. They didn't wish to make Sherry's potential vocation as a minister a bigger problem than necessary, but it was something she'd thought about for years, so it wouldn't be a good idea to close their eyes to its impact on their future together.

Together they read in the 1994 edition of the *Catechism of the Catholic Church,* on moral conscience, almost identical wording from what is in the Vatican II document on conscience, yet there were additional comments: "Conscience is a messenger of him, who, both in nature and in grace, speaks to us behind a veil, and teaches and rules us by his representatives. Conscience is the aboriginal Vicar of Christ."[3]

This quote is from a letter by John Henry Cardinal Newman, the Anglican who became a Catholic, not long ago declared a saint. Dee had found similar material from Newman referring to his conscience in his decision to become Catholic instead of remaining Anglican. Sherry remembered Dee sharing with her Newman's struggle over his decision.

Quinn and Sherry were wrestling with the idea of conscience, how that might get twisted, their growing affection for each other. Was Sherry's attraction to sacramental Christianity a matter of conscience? Was Quinn's tie to Catholicism about conscience or conditioning, or both? Could she, should she ignore any conflict she may have over one day becoming ordained, which is impossible in the Catholic Church while possible in the Anglican (Episcopal) Church.

Were they borrowing a problem from the future which might never become a problem in their relationship, or were they wisely looking ahead? This was their dilemma.

---

[3] *Catechism of the Catholic Church,* (1994), footnote 50, p. 439.

CHAPTER TWENTY-THREE

Erasmus

Ten days after the U.S. Capitol was breached by a mob, the Brunch Bunch met on the Kendricks' screened patio. Dee, Estelle, Francine, Monique, unanimously wanted to meet in person, not through zoom. Their urgent need to be with each other made them know what school children lose who work online away from their teacher and classmates— all the way through university students studying alone online, missing out on the usual richness of campus life.

The Brunch Bunch leisurely chatted while they ate, dining also on each other's perspectives and opinions about the current political climate; the extreme politics which had become an abrasive way of life.

Francine said we need more in public office like Erasmus five hundred years ago during the turbulent time in which he lived. She had a paper on which she'd scribbled notes, saying, "My memory isn't as dependable as it used to be and I want to share accurately some aspects about my friend Erasmus of Rotterdam, Netherlands, who lived 1466-1536.

"First, he lived through the Black Death plague just as we now have Covid-19, and second, he was a voice that mocked both sides of the

Protestant Reformation, which was a contentious period in his day, as is our present political polarization. We need talented personalities in and out of government, entertainers, script writers, comedians and such, who comprehend with complexity and courage both political sides today to help us see ourselves, our political selves, our political parties.

"With biting humor and piercing wit, Erasmus wrote dialogues, composed essays, used simile and metaphor and many forms of expression other than systematic argumentation (pure logic) to inform his readers. He was at odds with scholastic theologians committed to logical disputation:

> Traditionally, professional theologians were trained according to the scholastic method. The emphasis was on Aristotelian logic . . . Erasmus disparaged these exercises as training for intellectual sparring and unworthy of a true theologian, who must exert himself for the victory of the truth rather than a personal victory over the opponent in a verbal match.[4]

Francine continued, "Erasmus had a complicated life. His parents never married. His father may have been a Catholic priest. It is speculated his mother may have been a housekeeper for his father. Both parents died in 1483, when Erasmus was 17, from the plague. Erasmus died at the age of 70 from dysentery.

"It has been suggested money inherited for his upkeep may have been spent by those in charge of caring for him, who then placed him with monks, which led him to becoming ordained a priest in 1492 at the age of 25, though he seems never to have worked as a priest but ended-up with a fine education, including study at the University of Paris.

"Erasmus was brilliant, creating an edition of the New Testament in 1516, in original Greek, complete with study notes as well as corrections of Jerome's Latin Vulgate. He is said to have said he became a writer to correct the errors of those whose religion is usually composed of ceremonies and observances of a material sort and neglect the things that promote piety. He became famous for his biting satire, *In Praise of Folly*,

---

[4] Erika Rummel, *Erasmus*, (New York NY: Continuum, 2004), p. 27.

which attacked corruption in church hierarchy, yet he did not take sides with Luther and schism.

"He stood his own ground while buffeted from both sides: 'I am a heretic to both sides,' he wrote in 1522. He himself became the target of satire, as both Catholics and Protestants resented his reluctance to choose sides. He was derided as 'Errasmus'— Prone to error.

"Erasmus is labeled a Christian humanist, which means he advocated reading the great books, stories, plays, poetry of secular (classical) authors. He felt their writings aided human spiritual learning, which has been summed up in this way: 'Humanistic learning and human industry are required to receive the full bounty of the Spirit.'"[5]

"Erasmus was a free-thinking prolific writer, an independent scholar and educator who advocated reasonableness, tolerance, and conversation to resolve differences of understanding, rather than blind commitment. It was Erasmus's misfortune to live at a time of strife, when partisan spirit was valued more highly than intellectual doubt and when commitment was in greater demand than tolerance, which sounds like today, when party politics are valued more than cooperation, collaboration, or congenial compromise for the good of the country, the common good."

Francine continued, "Erasmus felt a well-rounded theologian must have expertise in the original Hebrew language of the Old Testament, and in the original Greek language of the New Testament to be able to discern mistakes made by translators and interpreters lacking linguistic skills. His translation of the New Testament from the original Greek is thought to be his utmost achievement in a lifetime of scholarship, writing, and teaching young males, as females were not yet often educated."

Francine elaborated, "I wish to concentrate on his gift of satire by referring to brain hemispheres: Using right-hemisphere inklings of humor, subtlety, nuance and intuition to experience and present all sides of an argument or viewpoint of his day, Erasmus was then able with his left-hemisphere language abilities to organize and express his original intuitions, cleverly, clearly and accurately, before reintegrating, returning to his right-hemisphere a new, transformed, whole insight; a synthesis involving both brain hemispheres. The words of psychiatrist, brilliant

---

[5] Rummel, *Erasmus,* p. 30.

author about brain-hemisphere differences, Iain McGilchrist, explains the process."

> There is a progress from an intuitive apprehension of whatever it may be, via a more formal process of enrichment through conscious, detailed, analytic understanding, to a new, enhanced intuitive understanding of this whole, now transformed by the process that it has undergone.[6]

Francine noted, that while Erasmus was able to grasp and lampoon the foibles and follies of both Catholic and Protestant positions at the time, he held substantial opinions. He accepted scripture as being sometimes ambiguous and obscure, while arguing that a literal understanding of the words and their historical context must precede any allegorical or spiritual interpretation. He felt Luther favored certainty not only in scripture but also in other things.

Francine added, "Remember, the left-hemisphere of the brain likes certainty." And then she made a final observation, "This Erasmus scholar I've been quoting inadvertently makes a brain-hemisphere distinction about Erasmus when she says, 'In his denial of the power of the human intellect to discern the absolute truth, Erasmus came closer to mysticism than to rationalism. The mystic admits his impotence and commits himself to God.'"[7]

Francine's last sentence about the mystic admitting impotence and turning to God, mystified Dee. What did that mean? Couldn't a rationalist do the same; admit being stumped and turn to God? Dee realized Francine had used the term 'absolute truth.'

---

[6] McGilchrist, edition 2009, *The Master and his Emissary*, p. 206.
[7] Rummel, *Erasmus,* p. 108.

CHAPTER TWENTY-FOUR

Judeo-Christian Myth

What is 'absolute truth' and how often does one look for 'absolute truth,' Dee asked herself, and then wondered whether we aren't always looking for Absolute Truth, even in our extreme politics these days. Dee knew: *though I may claim the U.S. Constitution is absolute truth in matters of government, and you insist the Bible is absolute truth in all of life, both Bible and Constitution must be interpreted. Hermeneutics again is the linchpin, the key-player, the cornerstone.*

Dee felt certain the hermeneutic of metaphoric discernment that unpacked the purple aura cat vision saved her life. She wondered whether a mythological hermeneutic might help save U.S. culture today. She tossed the idea to the Brunch Bunch saying, "These days we use the word *myth* to mean falsehood, which is not at all its original meaning. Myth does not mean false or fake. Why would Erasmus insist on a Greek translation of the Bible by creating such a translation himself? Let's say because he wanted to work with the most accurate version of the Judeo-Christian myth, which is a compilation of stories, recollections, history, poetry, and so on.

"There is a creation myth in Genesis, a mythical story about Noah, a mythical story about Jonah, and such. The whole New Testament is a mythic-historical story about Jesus. Why do I call them mythical? Because they are not like today's objective factual detailed reporting, yet they are truthful versions about life if we know how to approach them."

Dee was on a roll, "In a sense, science is our main myth today: our overriding story of life, death, and everything in-between. Before science, reason/rationality had become, increasingly for centuries, in Western Culture the overarching story to explain Life. Before reason, mythical stories told about creation, catastrophe, evil, suffering, heroes, gave answers to life's biggest questions, which may have brought a certain kind of freedom, some liberation from the heaviness of life, imprisoned by time until one day we die. Time and death rule.

"I talk with Oriana, my one-time sidewalk professor now in New York about whether today's political-conspiracy theories might be bastardized versions, deluded fantasies to fill a mythical void in culture now that the word myth has been degraded, devalued to the status of fakeness. It is true, the Judeo-Christian myth has become meaningless for many. And why?

"I say, the Judeo-Christian myth has fallen by the wayside, has atrophied by being put in a straitjacket of literalism, drained of its metaphorical richness, its symbolic depth, divorced from what speaks to us, profoundly, intimately, infinitely, *mythically*.

"For instance, Monique shared a sermon at Christmas about a 21-year-old man with Down Syndrome who became an athletic Ironman while his coach was *with* him, alongside him every step of the way throughout the grueling event. The Episcopal priest who wrote and delivered the sermon turned a real-life event into myth, it seems to me. He turned the story of this young man and his coach into how Christmas celebrates God-man Jesus coming to be *with* humanity every second of our lives."

Dee seemed unable to stop, "Recently I heard a sermon on the book of Jonah, wherein, as we know, Jonah is swallowed by a big fish where he remains for three days and three nights. What caused his being swallowed by a fish is that God asked Jonah to go tell the people of Nineveh, a large city, that it needed to repent. Jonah didn't want to do that, and instead boarded a ship and went in the opposite direction. A horrific storm tossed the ship about, sailors onboard tossed Jonah into the sea knowing he was the cause of the storm, and a big fish swallowed Jonah. Jonah cried out to God from the belly of the fish, Yahweh spoke to the fish which vomited Jonah on the shore and Jonah went to Nineveh and told the people to repent, which they did.

"Now, a human surviving inside a big fish for three days and three nights is fanciful, fantastical, not real, yet mythologically valid. The story of Jonah is a story, which can be extrapolated into psychological reality. For example, if our conscience indicates we need to do or not do this or that, or in some way we feel inclined to do what seems best, but we do the opposite, we can be swallowed into a sea of mental, psychic confusion and turmoil, nearly drowning in an abyss of emotional conflict, whereby crying out to our Higher Power, we are rescued, though on our own, without grace, we remain powerless to help ourself.

"I believe many molders of Christianity through the centuries became stuck in theology and traditional metaphysical language, unable to speak metaphorically, unable to engage mythologically. The mythological is not falsehood. However, blinded by reason and science, mythology has been dismissed as primitive, pre-logical, pre-scientific. Though this is true, myth carries weight in the big story of living and dying. I believe myth needs to be resurrected today; restored as a treasure trove of truth.

"I'd say the mythic is related to soul. Myth is fertile ground in which undefinable soul (psyche, interior experience, the inner life) can rest, where the soul finds meaning and purpose. Perhaps sleep-time dreams and wake-time visions are miniature mythologies." Dee could scarcely believe the energy alive in her as she said this.

Francine interjected, "Sherry and I have been looking at the Book of Revelation, the last book of the bible, which is a mix of two distinct topics: First, seven letters written to seven churches in his region which John seems to know well, in which he assesses the spiritual climate in each of the actual seven congregations. Second, his visionary material.

"Interpreting the visionary aspects of the Book of Revelation in a literal way would be like literalizing science fiction today. John wrote the book of Revelation while exiled on the island of Patmos off the coast of present-day Turkey. We might wonder if his visions were tied to the state of isolation in which he was living? Solitary confinement can cause such.

"More importantly, we might wonder whether our present-day widespread political conspiracy theories are tied to stress and months of isolation imposed by Covid-19, but even more, increasingly isolated from myth which for some time has come to be defined as falsehood. 'That's just a myth,' we say. Is the loss of myth now emerging crippled and deformed from neglect and abandonment, as Qanon?

"I'd say paying attention to one's sleeptime dreams is a way to restore personal mental health and the overall mental and physical health of the nation. Instead of tuning-into the internet to connect with political conspiratorial fantasy, tune-into one's own sleeptime dreams, phantasies of soul, personalized myths, so to speak. Paying attention to dreams takes one to the limits of what the I-ego-me knows, for most dreams, at least to some degree, seem baffling upon awakening from sleep to "me-ego-I" everyday consciousness. Dealing with one's sleeptime dreams helps stretch, enlarge, shape, enhance, grow ego-awareness.

"I do so love the title of the book, *Dreams: God's Forgotten Language,* by John Sanford, Jungian analyst and Episcopal priest. If only we could take this to heart to help heal the nation's political extremes, and our opioid crisis which will remain after the threat of Covid will have lessened.

"Discernment begins with one's own personal myth (questions about existence—being). Dealing with one's dreams lessens the tendency to place everything about oneself outside oneself, projecting personal fears, grievances, suspicions onto others, while feeling good about finding like-minded conspirators online as community, thus satisfying the human need to belong, to share intimate knowledge, so to speak, with others, while blindly falling prey to deception by cunning, crafty, power-driven untruth tellers and their untruths."

And then, it was as if Francine exhausted herself.

CHAPTER TWENTY-FIVE

Noah and the Flood

Estelle had been spongelike, taking in what Dee and Francine said about Erasmus, myth, sleeptime dreams, current conspiracy theories. Questions emerged in her, probably because she'd just finished reading Pope Francis' encyclical *Fratelli Tutti*. Estelle shared her questions.

"First question: has the Judeo-Christian myth which basically shaped Western Culture reached the end of its life? Or does it simply need to be reframed as myth and thus liberated from the confines of literalization?

"Second, do current political conspiratorial obsessions on social media, about pedophilia, drinking the blood of babies, eating babies, somehow connect with the death of myth? Is this strangeness the carcass of myth? And do these conspiratorial concerns about sexual abuse of children, mutilation of babies in anyway connect with the biblical statement: "Unless you become as little children you cannot enter the Kingdom of God." Now what does that sentence mean?

"Also, does our singular Pro-Life stance on the issue of abortion obscure massive multiple cultural pro-life issues beyond abortion which relate to devalued, "throw away" people, in the words of Pope Francis. For yes, we must remember, there is life after birth. Do those adamantly against abortion provide for unwanted babies after they're born?

"Third, does the term "deep state" relate to powerful matters below the surface in factions of the current collective mindset? Perhaps there are "deep" cultural tendencies some want to overthrow, which they find unworkable. I find this plausible, for I see that as wonderful as Science can be, it does not have all the answers we need to live and die well. The idea of Freedom, as vital as it is, does not have all the answers we need to live and die well. Prosperity, as fine as it is, does not provide all the answers. History, as informative and valuable as it is, cannot always show the way. Religion at its best can bring hope and help, but it too, has blind alleys, deep shadows, insufficient understanding, its own weaknesses, even wretchedness.

"And think about it, the conspiratorial-political concern about pedophilia, coming on the heels of the pedophile awfulness in the Catholic Church. I can't put it all together. Sometimes I wonder where is our hope today."

"And one last thing from the mention of Erasmus and humor, I've heard it said there is humor in the story of Jonah, where after Jonah did obey God and tell the citizens of Nineveh to repent, they so thoroughly repented that even the animals repented! Animals repenting is as preposterous as Jonah being in a fish for three days and three nights and the obvious exaggeration that Jonah goes by sea in the opposite direction away from Nineveh rather than by land to Nineveh as God is said to have told him. The story of Jonah seen in this light is humorous myth from which practical lessons can be plucked."

Then, there was quiet amongst the Brunch Bunch that day on the Kendrick patio. The house was empty. Zach was on a golf course, and Cynthia was with Pixie-Pickett at Sherry's. Much had been said here on the patio this late morning which had now slipped into early afternoon.

Strangely, Monique was quiet today. She hadn't mentioned beloved artist Marc Chagall. Was she not feeling well? Dee wondered if Justin had told his mother about himself and Cynthia? She also wondered if Francine knew through Sherry about Sherry and Quinn, and thus also about Cynthia and Justin. Dee was feverishly engaged inside herself with these possibilities.

Monique's attention was on a matter no one would have guessed. Not ever. Would she share this with her friends today? She was in the midst of deciding.

Francine was puzzling with Estelle's question, "Where is our hope today?" She wanted to help answer this for the group. The story of Noah came to mind, and insights flooded-in about the story of Noah as myth. Water in the story of Jonah, was even more important in Noah and the flood.

Within Francine, a tide of speculations, intuitions, inklings about the story of Noah rose to the surface of her mind. As if from her depths, she was swimming in a sea of profound metaphoric-symbolic understanding—more than her usual everyday mind could fathom—as if her mind was floating on top of an ocean of living waters, filled with currents of thought, emotions, living streams from somewhere inside her.

Francine was being filled with what poured into her, bubbled up, seeped into her consciousness, her awareness. She knew she had been stirred by what Estelle said about Jonah, by Dee having mentioned the possibility of today's political conspiracies as bastardizations of abandoned myth.

Francine remembered a book title from some years ago, though she hadn't read the book, *The Freedom of Man in Myth*. The title of the book stuck with her and made her wonder if myth does make humans "freer" in some sense.

With Estelle's comments on Jonah, one could see that myth can be freeing. Myth even frees us from the quantifiable rigors required in science and technology. Myth frees us from the systematic rigor of logic required in philosophy and other ways of knowing. Myth frees humans to live valuable life-lessons from ageless open-ended stories.

Quite possibly, today's bizarre political conspiracies, at their core, are grotesque distortions of lost myth. Also, out of today's shallow, superficial, simplistic state of psychological depth, toxic "wokeness" has arisen.

It was apparent to Francine that mystical Christianity began losing its mythical element as a literal mindset dominated, and today's politically-tied conspiracy theories might be tied to what has been lost in Christianity. The opioid crisis might also be tied to loss of myth, loss of meaning. Myth may not be factual, yet more comprehensively "true."

Francine began, "Take for instance, the story of Noah who built the ark for his family and animals to survive a flood that is said to have covered the earth. The story has much to say about our inner world, which can be flooded with unrecognized, unnamed longings and yearnings, feelings, hopes and fears, drowning in thoughts, unknown desires and questions—positives and negatives, an internal flow of the tension of the opposites.

"The myth starring Noah is about survival. Each of us is like Noah trying to figure out how best to survive physically, psychologically. Each generation has its unique survival questions and answers. Noah speaks to the present day, for he takes both male and female of each animal species onboard, just as I find the topic of masculine/feminine energy, qualities, tendencies, whether innate, traditional, or both, resonates with clients, which I often put into terms of brain-hemisphere tendencies and traits.

"Just as the vessel Noah built with divine inspiration and instruction, so too can a human become a vessel capable of withstanding the vicissitudes of learning about life hidden in the personality; seeking awareness of pushes and pulls from ancestry, environment, choices, significant others, culture, spiritual influences or lack of, unlived potential swimming around in each personality.

"Noah's wooden boat can be likened to another kind of "would" (the Will) as a factor helping keep one psychologically afloat as turbulent feelings and thoughts, threaten to drown us in worries, frets, fears. The role of Will, though limited, is important.

"With all those animals onboard Noah's ark, you can imagine the crap that would accumulate, which can easily be recognized as fertilizer, just as the crap we discover about ourselves brings growth, development, new life. Noah sends out a dove, a symbol of peace, which can be likened to indicators of becoming more peaceful with ourselves and others. Psychological healing.

"In the end, as in the story of Noah, there is a rainbow, we find the spectrum of a more colorful life, with shades of approach and understanding, contrasts, complementarities, less and less inundated with free-floating anxiety, drowning in feeling abysmal, we become increasingly a vessel capable of navigating Life despite what floods in on us from others and external situations.

"Something like this is what Redemption is about, why each person needs saving, salvation, a companion savior who has been through hell and back. I believe our hope is in the inner healing of each person, and thus the human condition, which it seems to me is the overarching theme of the bible, both old and new testaments."

And then, Francine did what she knew how to do well.

CHAPTER TWENTY-SIX

Monique Announces Sebastian

Francine paraphrased favorite quotes, from Swiss psychiatrist C.G. Jung's autobiography, *Memories, Dreams, Reflections.* Jung's father had been a pastor in the Swiss Reformed Church, so Jung the psychiatrist was well acquainted with Christianity. She put in her own words what Jung wrote in his 1961 autobiography, *Memories, Dreams, Reflections.*

> Christian nations are in a sorry state. Christianity has been asleep. Today, the Christian myth does not give enough answers to life's questions. The scriptures are not to blame, people are. Understanding the Christian myth has not sufficiently evolved in recent centuries. Rather, attempts to evolve meaning have been suppressed.[8]

Dee immediately thought of hermeneutics, the need to interpret scripture for this day, this time. Her interpretation of Jesus' parables was

---

[8] C.G. Jung, *Memories, Dreams, Reflections*, (Vintage Books, 1963), pp. 331-332.

her attempt to, balance while clarifying, the parables out of love for her aunt. Dee elaborated, "The old fourfold paradigm was ready-made for balance, steering clear of over-extending any one interpretive framework. The pendulum can swing too far, which seems to be a human tendency."

Dee spoke of the work of philosopher Paul Ricoeur who named two hermeneutic tendencies: a hermeneutic of suspicion, and a hermeneutic of faith/trust. Dee wondered aloud about Christians who dwell on the Antichrist and other doom and gloom, whether that kind of interpretation is coming from a hermeneutic of suspicion, while the Good News of Christianity shapes and attracts faith/trust. Each personality is influenced by its own dynamics. She knew this was too simple, but might hold some truth.

Estelle reviewed Pope Francis' encyclical *Fratelli Tutti*, as including both hermeneutics. His view of the Gospels for today's world, as brothers and sisters all, is inclusive, up-to-date, hopeful, while he also mentions human trafficking and other atrocities.

The encyclical includes history, democracy, the United Nations. He's spreading his net far and wide covering the tragedies of human behavior at this time as well as expressing hope for a better world based on the Gospels, the sharing of wealth, for which he's been called a socialist, because he advocates a world where there is land, housing and work for all. He's been applauded and criticized for advocating dialogue between different religions.

Estelle observed, "He's got to have broad shoulders to bear the criticism hurled at him by those who do not want so much inclusion." In contrast with the world-wide vision of the encyclical, Francine was thinking about a book with a single topic, the soul. Carl Jung's 1933 book, *Modern Man in Search of the* Soul. Today, such a book would need the title, *Postmodern Humanity in Search of the Soul.* In his last years Jung wrote, "Very few persons indeed draw the conclusion that the issue at this time is the long-since-forgotten *soul of man.*"[9]

Francine knew the Greek word *psyche*, soul, is in the New Testament nearly one-hundred times, which shows the importance it had for early Christians. Jung said the world is brutal and cruel, and at the same time

---

[9] Jung, *Memories, Dreams, Reflections*, p. 333.

of divine beauty. Which element we think outweighs the other, whether meaningless or meaningful, is a matter of temperament. He cherished the anxious hope that meaning will win the battle.[10]

Dee picked up on Jung's view that "temperament" determines our view of whether brutality or beauty outweighs life, strengthening her notion that the Book of Revelation is an apocalypse (a revelation), of hope, not a frightening prophecy. It is a mythical expression of cosmic reality, and should not be understood as imminent end-time warnings. The Revelation is, that while living includes strife, difficulty and turmoil, Christ is creative possibility, creative energy, grace, for overcoming every and all obstacles in the long run, if not immediately.

At that moment, Monique sat straight, clapped her hands twice, bowed to the other three, obviously impressed with what had just been discussed, and also a prelude to break her own silence, for she had something to share with her Brunch Bunch friends.

Monique announced, "I might have a man in my life. My reluctance to tell is I know Francine's poor regard of romance, but before your correction, Francine, I am compelled to explain, he is French-Canadian, which you can't disapprove, and my attraction is his handsomeness in my eyes, his *particular* masculine energy, and sharing the language."

It was quite unlike Monique to stop with such a brief description. The others inquired, "Does he live in Sandshell? Is he here on vacation? How did you meet him? Does he have a name? How did you meet in the pandemic? What is this particular masculine energy of his?

Actually, Monique's story turned out to be quite different than first appeared. From the start, Monique, along with near tears, explained. It seems, before the pandemic began, she'd met Sebastian Thwaites, close to her age, retired French-Canadian who'd owned a small construction company, relative of someone in Monique's office, and they'd gone out to eat twice before Covid came to town, whereafter he abruptly went back to Ottawa before country borders might close. Since then, they stayed in touch, phoning and texting. Extraverted Monique stayed in touch with many. However, according to Monique, as months of the

---

[10] Jung, *Memories, Dreams, Reflections,* pp. 358-359.

pandemic continued, the long-distance contact with Sebastian intensi-
fied.

To the Brunch Bunch it seemed incongruent that tell-all Monique
had never before mentioned Sebastian. Perhaps now in the midst of the
Canadian winter, and the social isolation from Covid, something intense
was brewing between the two of them.

As Monique's story poured-forth, it morphed into something else.
Essentially, it boiled down to this: now with vaccination against Covid
daily becoming more widespread, Christiane and Carter were settling on
a wedding date in June. This meant in a few months Christiane and Jameson would no longer live with Monique. She would be in her home alone;
an altogether dreadful prospect for her. As she spoke of this, tears rolled
down her cheeks.

She did not want to be alone in her house. She asked Estelle about
what it was like living alone since Reggie's death. Reggie, gone almost a
year now. He exited just before Covid-19 arrived, which seemed fortunate in retrospect. Estelle said she was OK with her aloneness, though in
her situation children and grandchildren were regularly in-and-out, plus
she had friends from former colleagues, contacts from years as a high
school counselor.

It was asked how Dexter is doing. Estelle said he is with his family,
not always harmoniously, but he is with them and he recently gave grandmother Estelle some advice after she'd texted him saying she'd gotten
vaccinated against Covid. He texted back reminding her to continue
wearing her face mask, despite the vaccination. She was amused and
grateful for his advice.

The rest of the Brunch Bunch that day was spent with Monique's
prospect of loneliness, Sebastian, Francine's defense of caution regarding
romance because it is not well understood and therefore the cause of
much pain, which she has often seen in her years as a therapist. Francine
said people expect long-term romantic bliss in marriage, which tends not
to happen.

Despite the long-term fragility of romance which Francine stressed,
Estelle was acutely aware of her ongoing bond with Reggie. He'd been
gone nearly a year, and she did indeed miss him.

CHAPTER TWENTY-SEVEN

Psychological Types

Estelle recalled when their eldest son was yet a baby, she'd mentioned to Reggie an adult education class at church during Advent on the topic of Christmas, and Reggie having never been around babies, though hopelessly in love with their son, while fairly clueless about what to do with him, suggested Estelle attend the classes, which she did while Reggie stayed home as babysitter.

Though after his death she could no longer apologize to Reggie in person, she did tell him now that she was sorry she hadn't understood him better—sorry she hadn't appreciated him more. She rather often told Reggie, now gone, that she was sorry about-this or-that, which didn't wipe-away memories of his shortcomings, just made them not as important.

To this day Estelle recalled aspects of the Advent classes at church when Reggie was babysitter. Such as, only the gospels of Matthew and Luke have Christmas stories and they tell very different stories of Jesus' birth and infancy. These Christmas stories, just as all of the Gospels, were written in hindsight about two generations after Jesus had died and risen, not at the time Jesus was born. While in Matthew's gospel, the birth of messiah Jesus is proclaimed with a star to Gentile magi; in Luke it is announced by an angel to Jewish shepherds.

Reggie did faithfully babysit each evening of the Advent sessions, Estelle remembered gratefully, tenderly.

While across town, Dee seated on the recliner in the family room, with a sheet of paper on a writing surface, was relating to a recent dream. She'd drawn arrows and written the *words thinking, sensing, feeling, intuiting.* These, she knew were four psychological functions in Jung's depth psychology. In each person some functions are more developed than others.

Dee knew she was most developed as an intuitive-thinker. She was less developed in the areas of sensing and feeling. She realized she may not have a professional understanding of these psychological realities, but she understood them in a way that made sense to her.

As an intuitive-thinker, ideas "came" to her. She didn't have an absolutely razor-sharp logical hair-splitting detailed picture of an idea, but she had uncanny speculations that occurred, arrived on their own, such as mixing fourfold exegesis with Jesus' parables. She saw the same in the computer writings of Matti, biological mother of Julia Montel in Kansas, who recognized dimensions of fourfold exegesis in Alcoholics Anonymous.

Dee recently thought about Matti and her prayer, "Please, God, help me not be fearful, lazy, stupid." Amused and amazed, Dee found herself convinced that to be complete, the prayer needed an addition. It needed to be "Please, God, help me not be fearful, lazy, stupid, or unkind." How could one in relationship with Jesus not be concerned about kindness. Dee felt she herself had slowly, over the years, become more compassionate—never prone to being particularly unkind—mostly aloof and unavailable to others.

Dee knew she herself was not cut-out to be a psychotherapist such as Francine who surely must be an intuitive-feeler, automatically connecting with people, knowing where they are coming from psychologically. Francine is also a clear thinker, but not so much sensate, as her library, office, and residence are not always in tip-top order. She struggles somewhat with five-sense everyday details.

Estelle, Dee would guess, is a sensate-feeler with a fair amount of intuition mixed-in so as to be able to relate to high school students, teachers, administration. Her sensate side shows itself in her ability to handle details related to the five senses. The ease with which her house is neat and organized. And her thinking is fairly well developed. Estelle is remarkably well-rounded.

Monique is a high feeling-sensate-intuitive, less developed in thinking. She knows people—what house they want, can afford, what might work best for them. She is scattered in her thinking, but highly effective in her job of matching people with real estate.

At the moment, Dee was concentrating on her recent dream. She used map-directions thinking, feeling, sensing, intuiting, drawn on her paper to relate to her dream in which a young boy fell out a high window on the south side of a building. At one point in her dream, she was travelling east. Using her map-direction-diagram of the four personality functions, she felt the dream was tied to less developed aspects of her personality—her feeling-sensate functions.

Dee did not use these personality functions as a "key" to put herself or others in boxes, strict categories, but the map-directions could be helpful as indicators if considered in a flexible way. The map-directions are valuable getting in-touch with one's most prominent approach to life as well as one's less-developed sides; potential waiting to become more developed; areas where we sometimes fall short, make mistakes, approaches to life in which we are less developed, comfortable and confident.

Dee had arrived at this "key" for herself: North=cold (thinking function), psychologically we speak of cold logic. South=warmth (feeling function), psychologically refers to feelings, being a people-person, knowing what's going on inside others. East=sun rising (sensation, sensing function), psychologically in touch with the five-sense world, detail-oriented. West=sunset, twilight (intuition, intuiting function), psychologically, easily experiences intimations, inklings, possibilities, speculations, inspirations.

Dee felt these dynamics mix in romantic attraction, and can also be why certain people annoy us. A high feeling-function might be irritated by, or attracted to, a high-thinking person. It's not simple. There are other dynamics like introversion and extraversion.

thinking / intuiting / sensing / feeling

Dee was amused thinking in terms of a recipe of flour, milk, egg, sugar. In one version of the recipe one egg is suggested. In another version of the recipe one-dozen eggs are used. Now, wouldn't that make a difference! Humans are too complex to be simplified, and so it is with relationships. Yet, a few psychological indicators can be helpful.

Take for instance, how we use our psychic energy as well as re-charge our psychological batteries. Extraverts tend to both use and restore energy from external persons, places, things, whereas introverts tend to both use and restore energy from their inner world.

Francine and her library helped Dee understand some of these ways of looking at the personality. Dee and Estelle had talked about whether Francine's unenthusiastic view of romance was a reflection of Francine's marriage, which she almost never mentioned, or was it indeed to help others avoid the disappointment of "being-in-love" fading after marriage while the relationship was evolving to more mature caring, affection. Perhaps Francine's reluctance about "in-loveness" was a mix of her own marriage *and* the pain and disappointment of romance she sees in her therapeutic practice.

Dee hoped Cynthia and Justin were talking about some of this, yet she and Zach hadn't done so. Zach expressed his attraction to Dee at the right time. But actually, he *met* her at the right time, when she was in the process of transformation.

Dee remembered suffering years of feeling she had no career. It was as if she had independent strength with no place to take it. Only in recent times had her career struggle diminished. Actually, after Reggie was put in the memory care facility, and certainly after he died, Dee was grateful for not being involved with a career as she was readily available to be with Estelle when Estelle needed her.

Dee found herself fulfilled despite not bringing home a paycheck. True, she had the inheritance from Tess. Not ever in her life did Dee know physical poverty. She had experienced loneliness, psychological poverty, psychological confusion that robbed her of worth, serenity, belonging. She knew what it was like to be massively incongruent with herself. However, that incongruence had quite nearly vanished. Her story was still evolving.

CHAPTER TWENTY-EIGHT

Justin and Cynthia Tell Monique

Daily writing their own stories were couples Cynthia and Justin, Sherry and Quinn. The latter two were talking about a June wedding, while Justin and Cynthia couldn't consider a wedding until after Christiane and Carter married, for they didn't want to clutter the calendar, complicate planning for Christiane's June wedding.

Cynthia was favoring a December wedding. That way, Charles, Kendal and Monty could come for Christmas, the wedding a day or two later, then a honeymoon someplace exotic to bring in the New year. Surely Covid would be under control by then with vaccine injections now already underway. She also observed, both seriously and in jest, "It will take until at least December for us to answer over 900 questions on the online worldwide Marriage Encounter website."

A Catholic Marriage Encounter usually takes place in a weekend group setting with other couples facilitated by a priest and two or three married couples, but not with social-distancing related to Covid. Cynthia was sometimes amused, other times annoyed with the questions, as well as Justin's seriousness about marriage. Sherry had perhaps been correct sensing his need for certainty.

When Cynthia brought up his concern about certainty in marriage, he said that was a big topic in his therapy. He didn't want divorce. He had scars from his parents' divorce, which Justin felt unmoored his father's fragile personality, though he's the one who broke the marriage, the family, and when his second marriage failed, he killed himself. Justin wanted to get marriage right—as right as possible.

Justin's therapist told him about the Marriage Encounter website. Justin was frequenting videos and podcasts of Bishop Robert Barron and Franciscan priest Richard Rohr, updating his Catholicism. Sometimes Justin and Cynthia watched a video or listened to a podcast together. He wanted her to know his interests so she wouldn't be caught off-guard after marriage, and he wanted to know her interests as well. Justin was remarkably attentive, romantic, not surprised when Cynthia resembled his mother's personality occasionally.

Overall, Cynthia decided Sherry was wrong that Justin was more interested in certainty than romance. He was a remarkably romantic partner, thoughtful in every way with Cynthia. She never stopped being amazed and flattered by this attractive, appealing, too-old-for-her male (they both laughed about). She'd been distantly fascinated with him for those many years while he had squelched affections for her, yet the attraction inside each for the other never disappeared.

Cynthia and Justin would likely not be getting married had Covid not ruined her job prospect in Kansas City. Then she would have moved out of Sandshell. They both laughed now about the age-factor; how it dissolved, uncovering this deep bond between them. The whole unlikely double-switch-scenario of Sherry and Quinn, Cynthia and Justin, oozed with unreal reality; uncommon delight. Monique, knew nothing of it.

Valentine's Day was on Sunday. Sherry and Quinn drove to Georgia that weekend so Quinn, Sherry's parents and siblings could meet. Her family was intensely aware Quinn was Catholic; had even studied a short while to be a priest. With her own father a minister in an evangelical church, couldn't Sherry have found someone else to marry; someone who would fit more easily into her family?

Quinn chose to sleep in a motel the Georgia weekend to have alone time during what he assumed would be a tense weekend. Meeting prospective in-laws would be naturally edgy, but with the religious mix, likely even more so. He and Sherry decided ahead of time she would not tell her parents what the two romantics were considering regarding their marriage and religion.

The weekend was far more pleasant and compatible than either Sherry or Quinn anticipated. Their mature compatibility brought comfort to everyone involved, who only knew that Sherry met Quinn through her friend Cynthia. The fascinating details including Justin were not told. That could be shared later, if ever. Keep everything as simple as possible, they'd decided, while Sherry was to meet Quinn's family in Indiana during Spring Break in March.

Back in Sandshell, Justin and Cynthia picked-up take-out food to share with Monique, Christiane and young Jameson. During Covid, Justin was in the habit of bringing food to his family since dining in restaurants was off-limits. The evening before Valentine's Day, Cynthia would be the surprise. Cynthia would be with Justin, announcing what Justin's family was to learn about their impending marriage.

After setting sacks of prepared food on the kitchen counter, Jameson ran into the kitchen, hugged by Justin and Cynthia. Next, came Monique, shocked at seeing Cynthia, "Ah, an unexpected delight," hugging the two of them," followed by Christiane and hugs and then Justin announced as if he were saying it's going to rain tomorrow, "I want you to meet my future wife." Monique said immediately, "I wish so, but you are talking crazy." Christiane stood stunned, somehow knowing it was not crazy talk, when Cynthia confirmed, "It's true."

Monique laughed, said, "Is this April Fool's Day?" clapped her hands, actually unable to comprehend this enormity, while instructing Christiane to get a bottle of wine as Monique collected wine glasses, and Justin told Jameson, "Cynthia and I are getting married." This was all so easy because everyone knew everyone. Yet, it was not quite believable.

Monique asked Cynthia, "Do your parents know?" and learned, "They do." It would be best if Monique not know Zach and Dee were aware since the day after Christmas, which Monique might not have liked—with her only now at Valentine's Day being informed.

At the moment there was the bustle of wine-getting, opening containers before the food was cold, microwaving what seemed to need it, and finally everyone seated at the table with Monique praying, "Thanks

God for this food, marriage news, and what else might be going on. Amen." Did she think Cynthia was pregnant?

Monique held court, "And what is this about? Tell me." Justin and Cynthia told everything including the Sherry-Quinn part, Justin's Christmas day proposal. Monique remembered Christmas Day when Justin and Cynthia went on a walk, which she remembered seemed strange. Christiane asked if they had set a date for the wedding. They told her either late summer or December.

Monique was grateful down to the soles of her feet grateful, that she'd remarked, "I wish so" after Justin said, "I want you to meet my future wife." Monique knew she might have said, "Are you serious?" with a wrong voice tone. Or, "Surely not," in jest while being serious. Or who knows what else. Monique knew things could float out of her mouth on their own accord. This time, the right words floated out.

Truth was that Monique had recently come to feel OK about Cynthia. But for a number of years Cynthia was not a favorite. Monique remembered her telling Cynthia about her own struggle with feeling powerless, and Cynthia made it obvious for some time after that she didn't appreciate the remark Monique aimed at Cynthia. But that was OK. As long as Justin was happy, and he did appear so this evening—Justin and Cynthia seemed obviously entranced with each other.

Just imagine, they'd had a secret mutual attraction between them for years, obscured and muffled by their age difference. Monique was once again puzzled by Life; the in-loveness she and Henri shared, the joy they had in their children, yet their marriage was difficult, and in the end, tragic. She knew Justin was in therapy and approved heartily. And then there was Christiane's first marriage that ended in divorce. Maybe marriage would go well for Justin and Cynthia. This evening, Monique would talk of her own current potential romantic interest.

She told of French-Canadian Sebastian, which was almost as amazing to Justin as the surprise sprung on her this evening. Christiane already knew about Sebastian. Monique talked about Francine's cautious view of romance, and added, "Even at my age I attract to masculine energy. Some would say, 'horny old woman,' but they misunderstand. It's more than that. Less to the sexual, more to overall male vitality; the appeal, the presence of maleness itself. I can't explain even to myself."

Monique knew the prospective marriage of Justin and Cynthia felt good. With Christiane and Jameson leaving the house in a few months, it was appealing to become formally tied to the Kendricks as "family." She couldn't have planned this better herself.

The next day, Valentine's Day, Monique spent the afternoon with Dee and Zach sharing the amazing marriage plans of their children, while Cynthia and Justin spent the day together at the beach.

CHAPTER TWENTY-NINE

Beach Tears and a Massage

The beach was getting crowded that late morning when Justin and Cynthia arrived on a weatherwise gorgeous Valentine's Day; people liberated somewhat from the fears and restraints of Covid-19. Overall, immunizations were taking place, hospitalization numbers going down, alongside decreasing pandemic deaths.

Cynthia and Justin found a spot to set-up camp for the day; sunscreen, drink, food, and a canopy so as to regulate the amount of sun or shade desired. Being together was thrilling contentment. It was a perfect day. Assembling and grounding the canopy together was lovely. Everything was enjoyable; being surrounded by people enjoying themselves, bright sunshine, temperature of 84 degrees.

They were aware of holidays in the past when their families walked the beach together, depending on the weather. Their shared families' history was fortunate, and even more fortunate their future together. Today they talked honeymoon plans.

Surely by December cruise ships would be sailing regular schedules, outliving the pandemic. A Mediterranean cruise in winter? If not a cruise, maybe the Rocky Mountains where neither had been, would be lovely in winter—a ski honeymoon, though neither knew how to ski. Cuba? The Caribbean? Mexico? South America? Their honeymoon days were limited because of her school schedule.

So far in their planning, the wedding ceremony would take place in Dee's parish church. Like father Zach marrying Dee, Cynthia accepted the idea of a Catholic wedding, but was not wanting to be Catholic herself. Brother Charles was enamored with chanting monks before he met Kendal, so it was natural for him to become Catholic.

Should Justin and Cynthia begin marriage living in Justin's Fort Hayden apartment, which is adequate? Should they buy a home? With realtor Monique that would be easy. With Christiane and Jameson moving out in June, Monique has mentioned selling her home and moving to something smaller with less maintenance. Canadian Sebastian may be a wrinkle in that plan. Justin did not take his mother's talk of Sebastian seriously. He telephoned Christiane who said she'd been under the impression Monique and Sebastian were simply friends communicating because of Covid causing Sebastian to remain in Canada. Christiane was surprised Monique made their relationship sound more involved.

If Monique sold her home, would Justin want to live in his boyhood home? How did Cynthia feel about that? There were positives like a big yard for children and pets. The home itself was roomy. Yet—it was packed with memories for Justin. Yet again—he wasn't sure strangers should live in what had been his home, full of links to his father. It seemed as if this gorgeous day had only questions.

Cynthia shared with Justin her recent trip to a bookstore seeking a birthday gift for Dee, and how her eye was captivated by one certain book, which Dee was indeed, now devouring, and how when Cynthia was in middle school, her family and Dee's parents, Cynthia's grandparents, took a trip to Scotland and the Orkney Islands north of Scotland so the men could play midnight golf. In a tea shop with grandma Paula, Cynthia spotted a book she bought for Dee, and Dee ended-up loving it, years later sharing it with Julia, Kendal's mother.

This brought up the idea of synchronicity, which Cynthia hadn't thought about for a while—maybe not since the night she watched the movie *Hugo* with Sherry, and then stepped into moonlight, which was a synchronistic experience.

At the moment, Justin was calculating that while Cynthia was in middle school traveling with her family in Scotland and the Orkney Islands, he was in college. Again, realizing how age circumstances kept them apart for years, their situation might well not have turned out so ideal.

Cynthia was presently concerned about grandma Paula who had been ill through the winter, not with Covid but the frailties of aging, multiple factors. Dee and Cynthia talked about going to Connecticut as soon as mother-grandmother Paula had her two Covid immunizations; perhaps during Cynthia's spring break.

Suddenly, there on the beach this Valentine's Day, despite the welcoming weather, beauty of the beach, joy of being with Justin, Cynthia was overwhelmed, needing to keep herself from tears. There was too much on her plate; honeymoon plans, where would they live, December seemed far away, would grandma Paula stay healthy long enough for Cynthia and Dee to be with her again? She looked away so Justin would not see her distress. However, he noticed, put his hand on her arm, asked what was wrong, she succumbed to tears, and needed to recover enough to speak.

"There's too much that needs deciding, too much up-in-the-air," she explained. He agreed, "It seems that way to me, too. So let's consider possibilities. We can do what we want, in the way, the order, at the time we want. We needn't ask anyone else, just ourselves, each other. He paused, and then suggested, "Let's marry as soon as we can." If he was jesting, Cynthia took him seriously.

And then, the air seemed lighter, everything began feeling better, more doable, when options were tossed up to see where they might land. An outline began to emerge. Obtaining a wedding license in Florida was easy; no blood test or medical exam necessary. They'd contact the church, and could report their interaction with the Marriage Encounter questions, not all 900 questions, but an impressive number of them.

They juggled possible plans around, until something plausible emerged. Perhaps Cynthia and Dee could visit grandma Paula in Connecticut during Cynthia's Spring Break in three weeks, during which time Justin would move from Fort Hayden to a spacious apartment they would choose in Sandshell where they would live, so he would drive to work instead of Cynthia. They would skip the idea of buying a home at this time. They would honeymoon at the end of Cynthia's school year and go someplace they both truly desired.

Cynthia felt better though her head, neck, and shoulders were tense. She put her head back, hands on her neck and shoulders. Justin noticed, and offered to massage the tightness, manipulate the near-headache away, as his dad did when Justin was young and upset. Justin's therapeutic touch increased the pain while relaxing the muscles. Again and again, his hands pressed against the tightness from the top of her head onto her neck, kneading the tops of the shoulders, down her back. She found herself holding her breath with the pain, and releasing her breath when the massage pressure lessened.

Slowly, slowly, she began to relax. His massage was the finest of Valentine's Day gifts. And then, after feeling she'd been luxuriously indulged, her welfare wondrously considered, asked Justin if she might give him such a massage. He said he didn't need such, he was fine. Cynthia flipped onto her stomach on the towel on the sand, arms under her forehead.

Justin sat next to her, his hands overlapping on his propped-up legs, looking out over Gulf waters which were part of him, his growing-up, his past, his assumed future. He felt congruent, complete, profoundly satisfied with the prospect of being with Cynthia being with him for the rest of their lives.

CHAPTER THIRTY

Genesis (1:26-27)

Elsewhere, Dee was once again consumed with puzzlement about the Holy Trinity. She knew the plural words in Genesis (1:26-27), "Let **US** make man in **OUR** image, after **OUR** likeness . . . So God created man in his own image, in the image of God he created him; male and female he created them."

Dee had heard a sermon in which it was claimed the plural 'Us' and 'Our' in Genesis 1:26-27 refers to the Holy Trinity. However, she found it more plausible that the plurality alludes to femaleness and maleness which is present throughout nature; the masculine and feminine. This was not her hunch alone, but one she found voiced from a Jewish-Kabbalistic view in a book that meant a great deal to her, *Androgyny: the opposites within* by Jungian analyst June Singer.[11] Why was this Genesis quote in a book on androgyny? That was *the* question.

Overall, androgyny involves the eternal flux of the opposing energies of feminine and masculine in everyone. These yin-yang opposites and complements are in every human being. Dee was grappling with why the Trinity couldn't be considered Father-Mother, Son, and Holy Spirit. The Holy Trinity is not in the Bible, but inferred from the New Testament by

---

[11] Singer, *Androgyny: The opposites within*, (2000 edition), pp.61-68.

the 3rd century. She found she could make the sign of the cross as usual, simply expanding the word Father to Father-Mother.

Since we today are experiencing emerging gender consciousness, no longer dominated by patriarchal ways of being, evolving into greater awareness, the Holy Trinity ought naturally to reflect this more complete discernment. And Dee looked again at myth in the words of Jungian analyst June Singer, "The myth-making process is always going on . . . it is our way of expressing ourselves from the inside out . . . Myth is the speech and the imaginings of the indefinable psyche (soul)."[12]

If myth is an expression of ourselves from the inside out, what are we saying today when myth has come to mean falsehood? Does this mean our psychological core is empty? There is nothing there? The traditional religious myth of western culture has outgrown itself; stagnated; no longer speaks from or to the depths of human experience? Dee sat with these questions.

She was struggling with the physically "virgin" Mary pregnant with Jesus. Need that be part of Christian myth? Was Mary's physical virginity now, in this day of science, viable or necessary as part of Christian myth?

Dee was acquainted with an older book, the 1973 book, *The Virginal Conception and Bodily Resurrection of Jesus*, by biblical scholar, Raymond E. Brown (1928-1998), a Roman Catholic priest, who wrote, "On the basis of the Gospel evidence it would be next to impossible to maintain that Mary would have been less holy if she had entered into normal marital relations with her husband and had borne Jesus through such relations."[13]

Dee never forgot she had no training in theology, not even a vital interest in theology, yet she had this ongoing, relentless inclination to tie Christianity to everyday experience. The idea of a virgin conceiving is a miraculous idea, but did it make Jesus more the Messiah, the fully human-fully divine Messiah? Dee continued to wrestle with Mary's virginal pregnancy. Dee never forgot Francine's understanding of psychological virginity.

She realized that apostle Paul's letters were written 50 or 60 years before the gospels and Paul describes Jesus as "born of a woman" (Gal 4:4) rather than as "born of a virgin." Mark's gospel is the earliest gospel

---

[12] Singer, *Androgyny*, (2000 edition), p. 62.
[13] Brown, *The Virginal Conception and Bodily Resurrection of Jesus*, (1973), p. 40.

and does not mention Mary's virginal pregnancy. Mark's gospel is the only Gospel that does *not* refer to Jesus as the "son of Joseph" or the "son of the carpenter," according to Raymond Brown.[14]

Dee read someplace that Mediterranean influence on the New Testament might have contributed the idea of Mary's virginal conception rather than Jewish heritage. Dee could live with that. She never forgot that Mary, despite patriarchal dominance, has been venerated in Catholic tradition.

Dee kept regarding the Holy Trinity as Father-Mother, Son and Holy Spirit. It needn't take centuries for widespread change to take place. Dee remembered Tess laughing about growing-up with the Holy Ghost, and returning years later to the Church and the Holy Spirit, not the Holy Ghost. The Holy Ghost had been renamed in Tess's absence. Change can take place quickly.

---

[14] Brown, *The Virginal Conception and Bodily Resurrection of Jesus*, (1973), p. 57.

CHAPTER THIRTY-ONE

Wedding of Cynthia and Justin

Change took place quickly for Cynthia and Justin who were married in the prayer garden outside Dee's church the first day of Spring, March 20. Before that, the prospective couple participated in a weekend group Marriage Encounter at the church where group dynamics and questions were socially-distanced creatively, meaningfully, which was an arrangement more fruitful than when just the two of them engaged the questions online.

Cynthia and Dee visited grandma Paula in Connecticut during spring break. Dee's mother was reasonably healthy but frail. While Cynthia and Dee were in Connecticut, Justin moved his belongings into a lovely apartment in Sandshell, which Justin and Cynthia had found together. Everything was falling into place for March 20, when their wedding would take place in the prayer garden outside the church, with recorded music.

Planning music for the wedding was primarily Justin's concern, for he was ardent about great and grand music. He could not play a musical instrument or sing well, however, in middle school a teacher ignited Justin's deep bond with fine music. Cynthia vaguely knew about his love in this area, but not really, not until spending time with him did she come to know he lived with grand sweeps of music in his car, in his apartment. The two spent time choosing music for their wedding ceremony.

On the day of the wedding, the processional music was "Jesu, Joy of Man's Desiring." At the time of exchanging vows and rings, "Ave Maria." And the recessional, "Ode to Joy." The overall simplicity of the wedding was embraced, magnified, brought to heights by these strains of music carefully, jointly chosen by the bride and groom.

The stickiest part of wedding planning was Justin's concern about Christiane's "ex" James. Justin wanted to invite James to the wedding, but it would have been awkward with Christiane's and Carter's wedding on the horizon. Justin had told James about his impending marriage to Cynthia and about their latent romantic interests ignored for years because of the age difference, which James seemed to find intriguing. Justin was reluctant to mention anything to James that might hang heavy with James, and Justin wasn't always sure what that might be. The two of them most often talked sports, politics, news of the day, the economy.

Justin had a soft spot for James who readily confessed to Justin how badly he'd screwed-up with Christiane and Jameson. Justin knew James's physical and psychological realities were burdensome and told Cynthia he wanted to continue to help James carry on daily in regular ways. She understood, agreed, and wondered how James could manage day-by-day with such regret. Justin said, "I have no idea how he does it."

The evening before the wedding, Monique had a yard party at her home to celebrate. Monique, after telling the group why she'd chosen a special song with diligence and a touch of humor about the age difference which might have kept Cynthia and Justin separated forever, played a recording of Maurice Chevalier singing the song, *Thank Heaven For Little Girls* from the movie Gigi, which Monique had proudly chosen.

The song nearly caused a stir when one female guest suggested Chevalier sounded like a pedophile, which greatly offended Monique, "I much doubt those lyrics in 1958 suggested that. Listen careful, the lyrics conclude, 'what would little boys do without them; thank heaven for little girls.'"

Drawing Dee aside, Monique urgently related, "One day you made mention a philosopher Frenchman on interpreting with suspicion or trust. Tell me quick in case I need it. What is his name, his idea?"

Dee sketched in a sentence the idea of Paul Ricoeur, who distinguished a hermeneutic of suspicion from a hermeneutic of trust/faith. Monique repeated under her breath, "Paul Ricoeur, suspicion, trust/faith," and now felt armed with information she didn't need, for the evening was quite lovely indeed; everyone eager to be breaking free from Covid restrictions, enjoying the good fortune of Justin and Cynthia being together.

The next morning at 11:00, Saturday, March 20, Cynthia with Zach and Dee at her side, followed by Charles, walked from the back of the church down the aisle to the altar where Justin, Monique and Christiane were waiting and where the two families hugged as family, whilst Cynthia and Justin were to be united in matrimony.

The parents were seated while Christiane positioned herself next to Cynthia as matron of honor, and Charles stood beside Justin as best man. They were indeed family—had been for years. Charles remembered his youthful crush on Christiane, and Cynthia cruelly teasing him about that, which now seemed long ago.

The bridal party was dressed informally. The bride, in a short summertime dress of white, with a hairpiece made of fresh flowers, wearing rhinestone sandal heels, carrying a half-dozen red roses to memorialize the six-year difference in their ages which might have forever kept them apart. The groom, dressed in a light blue open neck long sleeve shirt with light khaki trousers, light brown shoes.

Best-man Charles's pregnant wife Kendal and nearly three-year-old Monty, sat alongside Dee and Zach. Maid-of-honor Christiane's 6-year-old son Jameson, sat with his soon-to-be second dad Carter and two daughters, alongside Monique, Francine, Estelle, as well as Sherry and Quinn. Quinn had volunteered to be photographer for the day. Sherry and Quinn's wedding was only months away. James, Christiane's "ex" chose not to come to the wedding.

The music Cynthia and Justin pondered at length and finally chose for their short wedding ceremony, filled the air with tenderness, certifying, embellishing, sanctifying the vows, the exchange of rings, the words of the priest. Tears rolled down Cynthia's cheeks. Their small, simple wedding profoundly touched this close-knit group of people, who would continue the day, the marriage, celebrating in the Kendrick backyard with music, catered food, libations, deep human bonds as well as the presence of pets Pixie-Pickett and Bios.

One of Cynthia's hardest decisions had been whether to keep the name Kendrick, hyphenate Kendrick-Ammour, or simply become Ammour. This burned inside her and she didn't want anyone's input making up her mind. In the end, she decided she would become Kendrick-Ammour, knowing hyphenated names are bulky. She would continue to be Cynthia Kendrick in most instances, except on official documents. She might need to rethink this further, as such might have its own problems.

Justin and Cynthia left the backyard festival to drive further south down the beach to a destination not far away, where they would spend a week, as this was teacher Cynthia's Spring Break. Expecting Covid travel restrictions against Americans to be lifted later in the summer, they would plan a more distant and exotic summer vacation trip around the weddings of Christiane and Carter, Sherry and Quinn.

The Kendrick garden party continued without the newlyweds into early evening. It had been a most fulfilling day, which would come to be unfortunately, tragically memorable.

CHAPTER THIRTY-TWO

A Wedding and a Death

It was inconceivable, a wedding and a death in the same twenty-four hours. Life shouldn't happen like this, but then, humans have little control over much of life. In the night, Francine died of a heart attack, discovered by her daughter and husband, when Francine did not answer her telephone on Sunday morning, and they drove from their home in a town nearby to check on her.

Francine's death was a jolt. She'd seemed fine at the wedding followed by the garden party. Monique had driven her home that evening. Sherry was distraught beyond description, her mentor, lifeline, gateway to expanded worldview, therapeutic guru, was gone. Sherry was numb, paralyzed with grief, overcome with what seemed an impossible future. The Brunch Bunch, family and friends were dealt a stunning blow.

Sherry and Quinn were already dealing with heavy decision-making when Francine died. Francine and Sherry had talked about the possibility that the snake in the Garden of Eden is a way of expressing, talking about, representing low-level understanding; poisonous, toxic comprehension, interpreting situations, perhaps life in general, in too small a way, in the same way that a snake slithers on the ground. Francine's unexpected death brought only shock—no comprehension.

Sherry and Quinn had been grappling with religious affiliation. They'd come to the tentative conclusion they would be married in the Episcopal Church. Catholic Quinn would change church affiliation to the Episcopal Church, so that if one day Sherry wanted to seek ordination in the Episcopal Church that would be possible.

Quinn's tentative decision had been wrenching. Equally awful was the prospect of Sherry attending the Episcopal Church while he went to the Catholic Church. And then their children? In which tradition would they be raised?

Another possibility came to exist. Now, with pillar Francine gone, Sherry felt the full-weight of professional psychotherapy on her own, by herself, and the idea of pursuing a priestly future evaporated somewhat. Thus, marriage in the Catholic Church might be feasible—Quinn would not change church affiliation, and Sherry would decide to attend which church.

Sherry was familiar with sacramental Christianity through Francine. And now, with the possibility of the wedding taking place in the Catholic Church, it was as if a gaping wound in the relationship of Sherry and Quinn was stable and healing, at least for the moment. Yet, a final decision about the matter had not yet been made.

Sherry was also familiar with sacramental Christianity through Dee, while living in the Kendrick household as an intern. She remembered Dee's delight hearing a TV sermon wherein a psychological reference was made with Hebrew scripture that people today could relate to.

Dee told of the Hebrew people wandering in the wilderness. "After being delivered from Egypt, the people lost patience and complained against God and Moses, "Why did you bring us out of Egypt to die in this wilderness? We are sick of terrible food. Then, God sent fiery serpents that bit people and caused them to die. The people asked Moses to help them. God told Moses to make a fiery serpent and put it on a pole so that if one was bitten, he should look at the serpent and recover.

Moses made a bronze serpent, put it on a pole, and if anyone was bitten by a serpent, looked at the bronze serpent and recovered. [15]

Dee resonated with the psychological connection in the sermon when it was said that just as people bitten by the fiery serpent were healed when they looked at the bronze serpent Moses made and put on a pole, so too, it has been found in psychotherapy that *looking at* our issues—what works against us, what cripples us in our personality, what kills our quality of life—holding such up in awareness, looking at it at a *higher level*, from a greater perspective, helps make us whole.

It was further suggested a prayer that is always answered is a prayer requesting we see ourselves as we really are. Just as Christ on the cross said his executioners didn't know what they were doing, so too, we often don't know in the depths of our being why we do what we do. The more the personality knows its depths, the more fully one lives. Dee could never forget the healing and encouragement that came to her by way of understanding the purple aura of the cat.

The sermon that day concluded: "I feel certain that looking at a crucifix, asking the dying Christ to help us know our own psychological (soul) depths, is always answered. I believe we are given as much truth as we can bear, bit by bit. We learn what needs to die (be transformed, transfigured) in us, so that new life can emerge within."

Dee recalled the crux of what Julia's biological mother Matti wrote about that kind of knowing, the tension between Ego and Eden. Matti regarded Eden as an ideal psychological "place," state of awareness, when a personality is in touch with the Divine, whereas Ego is limited awareness of oneself and everything else; living by one's own efforts. Religion, at best, helps Ego find Eden. However, often, the platitudes of religion leave one with Ego alone, which results in fear, guilt, shame, worry and dread, or smug arrogance. Ego, at best, longs for God, wanting creative answers to why we're alive, what we're about.

Inadequate answers about living and dying can end in ego-exhaustion—mental/emotional depression. Addictions, compulsions, ideological fanatic-

---

[15] Bible Book of Numbers 21:5

isms, might well be misguided attempts to find satisfying answers to what matters most, knowing one day we will die.

CHAPTER THIRTY-THREE

Sherry's Snake Dream

A week after Cynthia and Justin's wedding in the prayer garden outside Dee's parish church, Francine's memorial service was held in the same prayer garden where Francine attended their wedding. Francine's cremains at a later date would be taken to Canada by daughter Clare and family for burial. Francine's daughter Clare and family wrote the obituary and with Monique met one of the parish priests selecting readings and recorded music for the brief outdoor service because of Covid.

Sherry contacted Francine's current and recent clients. Dee created a memorial brochure to be sent to friends here and in Canada. Monique and Estelle read bible verses during the private Mass. There was no reception following the funeral service, because of Covid.

The loss of Francine's fertile mind, profound intuition, commonsense wisdom, was keenly felt by all who knew her. Were there signs she had not been feeling well? Family, friends and clients wondered about that. She'd said nothing to anyone about her health, it seemed.

Sherry's day-to-day existence was most altered. Her daily loss was immeasurable. She dreamt the night of Francine's funeral:

I am fully adult though the scene of the dream is in the back yard of the house where I lived with my family when I was 10 to 16 years old, a house I liked, a place I liked. In this coming-of-age, pubescent place, I see a snake in the grass (low level ego) and expect Quinn to kill the snake. While he somehow does this, I immobilize the snake's mouth to keep it from biting by keeping the top part open, pushing hard with my right hand and then more importantly with my right forearm. There is thick fabric material between my arm and the snake's teeth which cannot penetrate through to bite me. I am not frightened but concerned while Quinn kills the snake though I am not sure how he accomplishes this. The snake has a spongy quality to it.

House: my frame of reference, not fully mature, but to my liking
Snake: low level of perception (ego)
Right-handedness: left brain hemisphere analysis can "handle" this
Forearm: already "armed" as in defense
Quinn: my contrasexual side – rational, analytic, sequential processing
Thick fabric material: self-protective, positive quality
Spongy quality for a snake: not healthy, no crisp demarcation, blurred outline

In waking life: I am not comfortable with my decision to be married in the Catholic Church. Feeling I would acclimate to the idea, which has not happened, I am perhaps dealing with this at a very low level of consciousness (the snake).

Sherry shared, "Francine's gift was to grasp greater and greater truth in a situation about oneself. One perspective she gave me is to not consider "in-love feelings" as the highest truth in the universe. I cannot forget at this time that I did not originally want to live in Sandshell, but in a larger city. I'm trying to look at everything.

"The religious denominational difference between Quinn and me may be too great to overcome. I look at Kelly and Paul in counseling, both raised Catholic, which she embraces, but he does not, that causes problems in their marriage. Raising children Catholic would not be comfortable for me. Perhaps I must face not marrying Quinn, and then move from Sandshell to a more metropolitan area. I must sit with this awhile, and discern before I act."

Dee wondered but didn't ask about literal Quinn in the dream killing the snake. What might that indicate? Why did Sherry not think about the flesh-and-blood Quinn in the dream? Had she been too symbolic, assuming Quinn in the dream represented her own analytical ability?

CHAPTER THIRTY-FOUR

Sherry's Predicament

Dee understood Sherry's predicament, shared the loss of Francine with Sherry, plus had her own regard for inner world phantasies such as dreams and visions, which she knew need to be scrutinized, neither overall dismissed in a lump as inconsequential, nor accepted too simplistically, Dee overestimated Sherry's ability to fully grasp her snake dream at this time.

The two talked about the snake in the Garden of Eden, as a way of talking about ego, our small-minded mind, our mind that thinks it knows more than it does. Just as a snake slithers on the ground, our ego-mind tends not to see far, wide, deep or high enough, but usually at a surface level.

A snake can slither up a tree or pole and gain some perspective, but for the most part is ground-bound, which is like us being held down by unrecognized personality dynamics: fear, anger, dissatisfaction, hopelessness, restlessness, insecurities, unnamed longing and yearning.

While the ego-snake can gain perspective, and thus "see" more, know more, outgrow its skin, so to speak, even climbing to the top of the tallest tree, gaining remarkable perspective, we still have a hard time seeing all dimensions and ramifications of a situation—we cannot see the future clearly—what we perceive tends to be limited and incomplete. This is the human condition; we are short on ultimate knowing.

In the Garden of Eden story, feminine energy (intuition) grasps our shortcomings and inabilities, and masculine energy (rational analysis) realizes this also, and we feel puny as we comprehend what we lack, which makes us feel naked, vulnerable, in contrast to Wisdom Itself. Naked Adam and Eve hid from God. Too little wisdom is a root of human struggle.

Earthly existence is an arena, a place and time allotted, for making choices, both our opportunity and challenge, also our sorrow and distress. Evil is creation gone awry, a collective composite of poor, pitiful, even atrocious choices made by humanity, a type of counterproductive to destructive collective energy. We are always struggling with the tension of the opposites.

However, divine grace is also energy, the antidote to poor choices. Grace makes life ever less stressful, more livable. This may be the overall message of the Bible: Humanity's need for Grace while Divine Grace seeks relationship with humanity one person at a time.

Sherry began seeing her situation in a new way since Francine's death, regarding both putting down roots in Sandshell and marrying Quinn. Francine's daughter Clare let it be known through realtor Monique that Francine's bayside high-rise spacious apartment was for sale first to Sherry who had right of first refusal, and secondarily to the Brunch Bunch at an attractive price. Sherry already had a verbal agreement regarding Francine's office and sizable library.

There were too many big decisions at stake. This was a watershed time for Sherry. Cynthia was newly married and not as available as before. Now, Dee was becoming Sherry's sole confidante. Sherry was relieved she and Quinn hadn't gone to meet his family during Spring Break. Perhaps he and his teacher-sister would go to Greece again this summer and thus blunt his upset of the breakup she was assuming might come.

Why was she concerned about Quinn? She needed to be thinking about how she would survive the pain of the end of their relationship. Yet, she couldn't find peace about Quinn becoming Episcopal, or her becoming Catholic, or having a mixed marriage with children raised in what tradition?

Sherry knew answers to why Christianity split in 1054, and countless times since 1517, but asked herself the questions again. Is it that different personality types experience religion in different ways? Historical aggravations from one era spill carry over into an entirely different era and exacerbate situations? Behavioral conditioning of children in their early years determine unexamined religious persuasions for life, creating tribal mentalities? Thus it is that religious splits continue generation after generation and are necessary?

She admired Quinn's mild cynicism about religion while he remained a religion-seeking person. For instance, he expressed amusement about monasteries on Mount Athos in Greece where women are not allowed, not even large female animals, yet the monks are dedicated to Mary, Mother of God.

Quinn does not hesitate to accept that humans create religion, males basically created Judeo-Christianity, along with most of what is recorded historically, which is only humanity's half-history with so little female inclusion. What would Christianity look like if women had birthed the bible, theological ruminations, church traditions? This is not the way things happened.

Quinn, as a biology teacher embracing the idea of biological evolution, accepts psychological, societal, economic, political, legal, technological evolution—everybody, everything evolves, including religion, and Christianity likely has miles to go before maturing into greater potential for understanding, let alone fostering the Kingdom of God Jesus talked about. Quinn is convinced humans have the potential to evolve into far greater spiritual awareness.

He assumed Francine was likely correct about her displaced spirituality theory at the core of romantic attraction, yet he himself was hopelessly "in love" with Sherry. He considered a recent comment attributed to Pope Francis that gays, though respected in the church may not be married in the church, is another application of St. Augustine's quote something close to "love the sinner but hate the sin."

Quinn wasn't overly-serious about religion, neither was he dismissive of it. He had a stance Sherry couldn't describe, or label. Perhaps his was a wholesome, inclusive attitude. He was about to further confuse her.

CHAPTER THIRTY-FIVE

Quinn Brings Relief

Sherry was befuddled these days, grieving over the loss of Francine. With her laundry, for instance. Since last washing her clothes in her apartment, she'd been unable to find a blouse which had been in the laundry. She'd looked everywhere, finally resigned to looking forward to where it would finally turn-up. A missing sock is not so unusual, found later in the fold of a fitted sheet or such, but she'd never before lost a larger piece of laundry. Days later she found the blouse stuck under a stack of folded clothing she'd put in a drawer, which was both amusing and confusing. Practical matters were too much for her these days.

She was overwhelmed with Francine's clients wanting to become her client. She did not understand Francine's confidence in her, including Francine's wish that Sherry have the right of first refusal to buy her bay-side high-rise apartment. Why did Francine want Sherry in Sandshell? Sherry was spread too thin, exhausted, needing to move from her beach-side apartment since that was Francine's arrangement with the owners. Is this why Francine opened another housing possibility for Sherry, giving her top priority to buy Francine's residence?

Sherry was too tired to be with Quinn. She needed to sleep every moment possible to have the strength to carry on. She mustered energy for conversations with Francine's daughter Clare, dealing with practical matters that led to talk about Francine.

A Saturday, several weeks after Francine's death, Quinn suggested he bring food, which they enjoyed that evening on the balcony which soon would no longer be Sherry's home. Quinn brought relief to anguished, exhausted Sherry. After listening to her present overextended circumstances beyond her control as they ate, he said when finished with the food and a glass of wine, "Let's walk on the beach," which they did this lovely evening with clear sky, remarkably fine temperature, bare feet soothed in comforting sand, walking hand in hand, they were quiet.

After taking in the enormity of sea and sky, day beginning to rest in night, Quinn began, "Our mixed-marriage problem need no longer be a problem." Sherry did not begin to comprehend, only automatically uttered, "Oh?" He responded, "A path seems to have cleared." Clearly puzzled, she declared, "I don't understand." He hesitated, "Do you want there to be a way?" She took not another step, but turned to him, "Well, of course, obviously, without a doubt, but it seems so impossible," aware of sounding desperate.

Quinn did not verbally respond. They hugged tenderly, two tiny specks embraced in the vast beginning darkness, aching for each other, held in the grip of mature desire including, yet beyond, physicality.

Quinn began slowly, "In good conscience, with clarity of mind, after initial discernment, I am feeling more able to join the Episcopal Church. I want never to turn my back on the Catholic Church and what it has given me. I feel I can cherish both faith traditions. I need not live with an either/or attitude. It is Christ who is the crux and core, the source of what I depend on. The Episcopal Church includes sacraments, and in general, what is important to me. Episcopal priests are accepted as priests in the Roman Catholic church, even if married."

She wanted to be sure, "You would join the Episcopal Church so our religious practice would coincide, be in agreement, we could share?" "Yes," was all he said.

In her gut, Sherry reverberated with the fact that Quinn killed the snake in her dream. She should have thought of flesh-and-blood Quinn as well as symbolic Quinn in the dream! She told Quinn her dream and her reactions to it. Perhaps a path had opened. There was a way for them to share life together.

She asked how his family might react. He felt confident, "My family respects that I am an adult, by nature a religious-type, neither frivolous nor fanatical, but reasonable, committed with clarity. They know I am a cautious sort; I walk through things before I am convinced; like going to the seminary to learn I did not have a priestly vocation. I'm not a risk-taker for the most part. Sherry marveled at her snake dream. Quinn had insightful comments tied to the fourfold exegesis Dee used with Jesus' parables. Sherry saw the usefulness of the fourfold paradigm in dream interactions. Quinn remembered seminary material about the limits of allegorizing, stretching metaphors beyond their limits to situations that do not fit. He remembered a Protestant theologian who advocated using the literal sense with scripture unless the literal sense leaves one in the dark, or the text literally understood, says something unworthy of God.

He remembered learning of a Roman Catholic theologian convinced that metaphor was a central clue to better understanding religion and that if you eliminate metaphorical language in religion, you change human reality. He recalled Thomas Aquinas in *Summa Theologica* wrote that when Scripture speaks of God's arm it doesn't mean God has an arm, but it is a way of speaking about his "operative power."

Quinn was acquainted with long-ago allegorically inclined Jewish Philo, and most especially Christian exegete Origen. He knew the names of John Cassian and St. Gregory the Great, thought to have largely contributed to the medieval doctrine of the four senses. Cassian used four biblical meanings of Jerusalem as an illustration: the actual city, the church on earth, the human soul, and the heavenly city, our final home.

Sherry was impressed with Quinn's recall. He replied, "The Episcopal church nurtures the tradition of solid, accurate church history, which I find vital." Sherry realized it was unlikely she would ever again forget to look at a dream literally, as well as metaphorically/symbolically. She looked at her snake dream from the perspective of flesh-and-blood Quinn whom she wanted to marry, who with his talk of joining the Episcopal church was killing her low-level assumptions about the impossibility of their marrying.

She thought more about the spongy snake, the blurred nature of low-level comprehension going on in her at the time, and the crispness, sharp outlines of what Quinn just said about his new-found freedom to join the Episcopal church. She needed to get smarter about dream images. She felt certain Francine would not have made her mistake; a thoughtless oversight. Dee had noticed Sherry's oversight regarding the dream. Sherry had forgotten to consider it literally, as an external event—Quinn killing the snake—ending their religion quandary.

However, the snake dream had more to offer.

CHAPTER THIRTY-SIX

Quinn's Convictions – Clare's Comments

Sherry and Quinn talked at length about his joining the Episcopal church. Quinn admitted to himself and Sherry he had long been at odds with the Roman Catholic position against artificial birth control, imposed by celibate males—which is incongruent, almost amusing, but not really, because of enormous consequence.

Likewise, he sees as grossly inconsistent, even hypocritical, that married Episcopal male priests are accepted as priests in the Roman Catholic Church, while celibacy is still required for young ordinations; exceptions are older widowers.

Quinn told how he struggled with the annulment process required of divorced Catholics, and the male-only priesthood. These are some of the reasons he could not become a priest.

He found himself comfortable with everything about the Episcopal church as sacramentally, liturgically on the same page with the Roman Catholic church. Having close Episcopalian friends, he's been to baptisms, funerals, weddings in the Episcopal church. He does not expect the Episcopal church to be perfect just as the Roman Catholic church isn't perfect. They are flawed human institutions.

In the midst of all this, Sherry was learning from Francine's daughter, Clare, about Francine's skeptical view of romance. Yes, years of seeing the pain of unhappy marriages in psychotherapy was a factor, but there was something closer to home. Clare's father, Francine's husband, was not a model husband.

Clare summarized, "My father was a better father than husband. I see that now. He was a flashy-type, with a narcissistic tendency. My mother seemed to adore him, while he took her for granted. I believe she wanted more of his attention and affection. He was a journalist with a flair, who smoked himself into lung cancer and died when I was in my late twenties. She will be buried next to him, as she requested.

"He was a superb journalist who made journalism his first love. Everyone else came second. I felt loved by him. However, I wonder as I've gotten older looking back, whether he assumed my mother was so self-sufficient she didn't need more of him from him. I have come to consider the possibility that she was chronically disappointed in their relationship."

Sherry carefully processed Clare's words about her mother being chronically disappointed in her marriage, combined with Francine's cautionary view of "being-in-love" as a kind of displaced spirituality. Had Francine sublimated her own unmet love-needs to "being-in-love-with-Being?" If this was so, was it unusual, unhealthy, or wise?

Clare admitted she might be wrong about her mother's disappointment in her marriage. "There was much I didn't and don't understand about my mother. She seemed to have almost too many interests. Perhaps my father felt slighted by her numerous interests, such as early church history, as you can see in her extensive library. She regretted she wasn't formally trained in theology. She felt tentative, unsure about her self-education in these areas. Yet her fascinations with them remained." Sherry knew Francine felt unsure of herself in these self-taught areas, for she easily said so.

Clare was a genteel personality, attractive with a flair about her, a high school French teacher. She was warm, inviting, eager to share about her mother, drawn to Sherry, the Brunch Bunch, and their closeness to her mother Francine. Only Monique had met Clare over the years. Francine had been close-mouthed about her marriage, even with Monique.

Francine never met Quinn, though Sherry told Francine about him. Francine had known Sherry and Justin were dating before Justin and Cynthia married. It was then that Sherry took concrete notice of Francine's wariness about "being-in-love," romantic attraction. As if Francine hoped to help lovers know "in-love" emotional bonds would one day dim and need to evolve into something more substantial, more truly loving.

Partly, for Francine, "in-loveness" was, at its core, about mating, physical survival of the species, while "loving" another involved a more transcendent quality tied to lifelong commitment between two limited and incomplete humans.

Sherry knew Quinn's decision to join the Episcopal church might have unforeseen consequences down the road. Would he one day blame her for his leaving the Roman Catholic Church? She took solace that he knew the priesthood wasn't for him years before the two of them met. So, earlier he had discerned, and now readily admits, issues he had with the church before Sherry was in his life.

Amidst all this, a decision needed to be made by Sherry whether to purchase Francine's bayside high-rise condo. It was a small unit, more adequate for one person than two. Monique let it be known she was eager to purchase Francine's condo, for then Justin and Cynthia could purchase her house which she would happily vacate after Christiane and Carter marry. When Monique's house would feel empty without Christiane and Jameson. Monique was juggling the situation to meet her own needs.

Palm Sunday came, and then because of Covid, Quinn watched Holy Week Services online from the Vatican. The Easter Vigil on Saturday evening was for years Quinn's most meaningful observance of the year, which he would watch online this evening with Sherry.

Holy Saturday, Quinn and Bios went on an extended early morning run-walk. Sherry spent these final days in her apartment sleeping as late as possible to recover from the exhaustion of the loss of Francine, and the huge fallout of her death. Sherry had a most helpful dream that would help her through this raw time. This dream was much more transparent to her than her snake dream.

In this dream, two themes were present: a Russian scenario and a sexually transmitted disease theme. Sherry quickly transposed the two:

Russian=rushin'; sexually transmitted disease=intimate, private dis-ease. She concluded: "In my inmost being, I am infected with dis-ease, stress, feeling rushed."

As days went by, she was able to assess, "The dream helps me focus on one thing at a time, whereby I maintain a more sane, calm emotional state, accomplishing more in a timely way." Recalling her "rushin' disease" dream helped her recalibrate herself again and again during this time of loss and change.

Quinn's possibility of joining the Episcopal church had led him to begin reading, more thoroughly, Vatican Council II documents. On this splendid Holy Saturday morning, running, walking, contemplating his future, he and Bios strolled through a Methodist Church's "Meditation Walk" a lovely, landscaped space between some of their buildings and part of that walk included the Stations of the Cross, familiar to him with his Catholic background.

But then, he'd once prayed the Stations of the Cross in an Episcopal church with friends. Quinn had long been an ecumenical Catholic. Christianity, indeed, the world at large, needs ecumenism, which means Christian unity with diversity, without animosity. Quinn had this recognition before he'd ever heard the word ecumenical.

He felt it in Greece, too, the commonality between Catholic and Orthodox Christianity. None of this was alien to him. He'd lit candles for family and friends in an Orthodox Church when he was in Greece. He'd attended Orthodox Mass in this country, with a friend. He was naturally ecumenical, which was becoming ever clearer to him.

CHAPTER THIRTY-SEVEN

Quinn and Dee Talk

Quinn and Bios this early morning Holy Saturday, the day before Easter, were intentionally jogging down the familiar street of Zach and Dee Kendrick, where Dee was in the backyard fresh air with glorious sunshine beaming radiant over thriving plants. Quinn hoped Dee would be in her opulent back yard, and there she was, soaking in the splendor of the morning.

Quinn and Dee happily spotted each other at the same time. Dee invited Quinn and Bios into the yard, where Bios eagerly had a drink of water and rested in the shade. Zach was on a golf course. Conversation quickly became consequential—about Sherry and how was she faring after Francine's death, which led Quinn to introduce to Dee his prospect of joining the Episcopal (Anglican) church; how he'd been reading Vatican II documents on ecumenism and religious freedom, which he realized did not include leaving the Roman Catholic Church to join another denomination for the sake of unity. He clearly understood that.

He questioned, "Whether a stark either-or frame of mind is the only available attitude; you are either one denomination or other. Isn't it possible to wholeheartedly embrace more than one denomination at a time?

Might that be ecumenism at its fullest? Realizing I get this, this, and this from one group and other attributes, insights and inspirations from another group."

Dee countered, "Perhaps it boils down to the practice and practicality of attending more than one church, contributing financially or otherwise to more than one group. I wonder if, over time, one denomination would naturally become one's preference. Maybe it's like having several enduring relationships but no exclusive relationship. I don't know if that's a good analogy."

Quinn thought about the analogy, "I'm not sure. An exclusive relationship between two individuals is far different than exclusive affiliation with a group. A group will likely not be devastated or destroyed if a member shares affiliation with another group, whereas having simultaneous intimate affiliations with others tends to ruin a one-on-one relationship," Quinn smiled with his understatement.

"Further, it seems to me a group or institution is at least partly defined by its differences from other groups. Catholic is different from Protestant, and so on. Ecumenism is not absolute melding one into another but recognizing and appreciating similarity more than emphasizing dissimilarity.

"I guess the question is whether an individual can comfortably embrace the outlook and practices of two denominations simultaneously over the long haul. You are likely correct that over time one or the other denomination would win one's heart, affections, allegiance. However, denominational difference is healthy and inevitable because religion is vast, largely incomprehensible. Now, with worldwide communication available, people more readily pick and choose religious traditions, and integrate aspects of other denominations, traditions, practices."

Dee changed the topic somewhat, "Or people choose religious traditions less and less. Period. It all depends on whether *myth* survives, now that myth popularly means falsehood. Yet, I see ever more clearly, myth as right-brain-hemisphere understanding, comprehension, neither scientific or strictly analyzable in left-hemisphere style. The Judeo-Christian myth is an overarching story about living and dying. It's the story of evolving human beings aware of Being."

Quinn was impressed with Dee's talk of beings and Being; the revival of myth as a valid way of knowing, uncovering truth. She elaborated, "Christianity has one foot in linear (chronological history) and the other foot in cosmic/mythical (kairos reality).

Dee shared, "I've just finished reading a visually beautiful book with over a hundred color images, an intriguing 2018 book Cynthia gave me for Easter, with the title *Resurrecting Easter*, best summed up as "How the West lost and the East kept the original Easter vision," by historical Jesus-scholar, John Dominic Crossan, and his veteran photographer and visual artist wife Sarah Sexton Crossan."

Dee invited Quinn and Bios into the screened patio where the book was lying on the table where she'd been again looking through it. Its gold background cover of resurrecting Christ within a mandorla symbolizing his human/divine nature, liberating Adam and Eve symbolizing all of humanity, by holding onto their wrists, releasing them from Hades (death in myriad forms). She picked up the book, finding certain pages and reading aloud,

> The Eastern image of Christ's universal resurrection is in closer conformity to and continuity with the original Christian-Jewish meaning of 'Resurrection' than is the Western—contradictory—image of Jesus's individual resurrection (p. 175).

> [Just as] Jesus's kingdom of God . . . is already present but only if, when, and as humans accept it, participate in it, collaborate with it, enter into it, and take it up themselves. It is, in other words, a process over human time and not just an instant in divine time (p. 174).

> [So too, Christ's resurrection was not] a special, individual privilege for him alone . . . [but] something far, far greater than that . . . it is not an instantaneous event . . . [though] it begins with Jesus, but cannot be individual for him alone. It must be universal for all those who have died before him. Easter is not an individual

'Ascension' for Jesus, but the start of the universal 'Resurrection' with Jesus (p. 174).[16]

Dee said, "I can't yet explain this well. I need to sit with it awhile for its depths to penetrate and saturate my understanding. The book is too profound to be grasped without studying its implications. The book's last chapter is jaw-dropping, using the word *postcivilization* connected to military weapons now available, capable of destroying civilization as we have come to know it. The book presents a unique view of civilization."

Both Dee and Quinn were quiet externally. Internally however, Dee remembered 1054 as the most common date cited of the East-West split in Christianity. She needed to re-read the book with this date more fully present in her mind.

Quinn was partially listening and paying attention to what Dee was saying, while at the same time, remembering in his edition of Vatican II documents,[17] it is stated: "The Anglican communion occupies a special place," in which catholic traditions and institutions continue in part, from the time of the Reformation.

He could not stop thinking about Sherry, the feasibility of marriage and its impossibility. Dee spoke, pointing to the cover of her Easter book, "Here we see Christ grasping Eve's wrist as well as Adam's wrist with his other hand. The book's art work shows this was not always the case. In earlier images, only Adam's wrist was directly grasped by Christ, which surely must have symbolized all of humanity, but it is only later that Eve's wrist is also directly grasped, portraying, acknowledging evolving human awareness of the female, the feminine in Christianity."

Dee's comment landed squarely on Quinn's marriage dilemma, no women priests in the Roman Catholic church, which opened a floodgate of what he'd been reading in Vatican II documents.

---

[16] Crossan, *Resurrecting Easter,* (2018).
[17] Vatican II Documents, Austin Flannery, O.P., general editor, (1996) p. 513.

CHAPTER THIRTY-EIGHT

All-Inclusive Caring Christ

In Quinn's edition of Vatican II documents he read: "It is up to everyone to see to it that women's specific and necessary participation in cultural life be acknowledged and developed (p.237)." Why not in church hierarchy, in ordination? Quinn asked himself. Further, Quinn found in the documents,

> Truth can impose itself on the human mind by the force of its own truth, which wins over the mind with both gentleness and power (p. 552). [Humans] are also bound to adhere to the truth once they come to know it and to direct their whole lives in accordance with the demands of truth (p. 553). The individual must not be forced to act against conscience nor be prevented from acting according to conscience, especially in religious matters. The reason is because the practice of religion of its very nature consists primarily of those voluntary and free internal acts by which human beings direct themselves to God (p. 554). God calls people to serve him in spirit and in truth . . . God has regard for the dignity of the human person which he himself created; human persons are to be guided by their

own judgment and to enjoy freedom (p. 560). Conscience is people's most secret core, and their sanctuary. There they are alone with God whose voice echoes in their depths (p. 178). In Christ and in the church there is, then, no inequality arising from race or nationality, social condition or sex, for "there is neither Jew nor Greek; there is neither slave nor freeman; there is neither male nor female. For you are all one in Christ Jesus" (p. 50) from Gal 3:28.

Quinn was in turmoil. Anguished. Could he keep his bond with the Catholic Church while joining the Episcopal Church? Was he being dishonest with himself? Equally, it seemed damaging, unhealthy, to forsake his attraction, affection; the mutual liking and longing he and Sherry had for each other. At core was relationship with Christ Jesus, not institutional affiliation, yet . . .

After Quinn and Bios left Dee to continue their run, she remained on the patio looking at pictures of paintings, coins and other artifacts in the Easter book, taking special notice of paintings in which the Christ figure is trampling down locks, keys, bars and bolts in Hades-as-death, which made her think of human contrivances that keep us locked into destructive behaviors individually and collectively, while we yearn for and need personal, relational, universal harmony. We desire peace with ourselves, others, and peace on earth, yet the seemingly available keys often don't appear to work.

The Easter book speaks of the Iron Age and what it has ironically brought to so-called civilization as tools and weapons. Dee began thinking of psychological defense mechanisms, machinations that work for and also against harmonious existence; unconscious factors, our unawareness, the unknown dynamics at work in each of us which need transformation; healing bringing harmony.

Dee saw in Christ's trampling down Hades in the art work of the Easter book, his freeing, his liberation of evolving humanity. This Easter book highlighted for Dee, Pope Francis's term "throw away people" in his encyclical, *Fratelli Tutti*. She clearly understood there are no "throw away" people, not in the dim past of history or throughout the centuries, not from any geographic place or situation. No one is outside of, or beyond, the cosmic caring concern of Christ.

The central idea in the Easter book is that Easter is not about Christ's individual resurrection, but universal resurrection, which is an ongoing process, not a single event. Dee remains grateful Cynthia found this book for her, a visually beautiful book uniquely researched, requiring that one sit with what it says about the Messiah myth of Christianity. Awareness by Christ's friends both now and when he'd been living on earth with family and friends, of his post-death presence.

CHAPTER THIRTY-NINE

Snake Dream – More on Death

Sherry came by the Kendrick home a few evenings after Easter to talk further with Dee about her snake dream. Zach was helping Cynthia and Justin assemble a piece of furniture at their house. Zach had a knack for this kind of activity.

Sherry refreshed Dee's memory of her snake dream:

I am fully adult though the scene of the dream is in the back yard of the house where I lived with my family when I was 10 to 16 years old, a house I liked, a place I liked. In this coming-of-age, pubescent place, I see a snake in the grass (low-level ego) and expect Quinn to kill the snake. While he somehow does this, I immobilize the snake's mouth to keep it from biting by keeping the top part open, pushing hard with my right hand and then more importantly with my right forearm. There is thick fabric material between my arm and the snake's teeth which cannot penetrate through to bite me. I am not frightened but concerned while Quinn kills the snake though I am not sure how he accomplishes this. The snake has a spongy quality to it.

"Before, when we talked about this dream, I ended feeling I made the mistake of *not* regarding Quinn as literally, physically, actually Quinn. However, I have since come to realize that was not an error. My shortcoming with the dream was not exploring dream-image Quinn more fully, symbolically. Considering Quinn as my ability capable of killing off toxic low-level ego-understanding. Since then, I have approached the Quinn dream image as left-brain-hemisphere perspective for validating, testing, qualifying and verifying whatever. My right hand and forearm (left-hemisphere) pushing against the snake's mouth to keep this low-level perspective from biting into me, my overall understanding.

"Further, the dream scene (house, frame of reference) suggests I am in an immature "place." In the end, left-brain analysis prevails over the blurry, ill-defined, potentially toxic issue at hand whilst I (ego) am adequately protected by material, perhaps the fabric of what I already know.

"What I know is Francine believed I am gifted as a psychotherapist, so why must I become a minister? To be like my father, which is misplaced, ill-conceived in me. Francine's library introduced me to early Christian history. Interpreting the bible exponentially is now part of who I am, and I have a sacramental mindset, a respect for myth. You, Dee, have helped form who I have become. I've only to analyze my situation as it has evolved to dispel the notion that becoming an ordained minister must be in my future.

"Francine's death took her away as a shield I needed to grow into carrying the task of soul-healing, but now I must continue to grow into that responsibility on my own with the help of Divine Grace. There may be more I can learn from this dream, but I feel satisfied for the moment. Dreams always offer more than we can discern. Perhaps they come to invite us to ask new questions, to remind us of how little we know."

Dee saw again the power of symbolic understanding, the role it plays in everyday life. The abundance of possibility it provides. And she was filled with peace.

Meanwhile, Zach was with Cynthia and Justin at their apartment putting together a quaint corner curio with glass shelves and mirrored interior which Cynthia ordered online after it caught her fancy. She planned to paint it in a distinctive way as yet undecided. The ornate piece of furniture would move with them to Monique's house should Monique purchase Francine's high-rise condo if Sherry declined it for being too small for Quinn and her; another big decision on Sherry's shoulders. Not her decision alone, yet ultimately hers.

As the evening with Zach, Cynthia and Justin progressed, Cynthia was explaining her fears about death, fueled by Francine's recent death, and the fragile health of grandma Pauline, Dee's mother, whom Cynthia and Dee visited during Spring Break. Justin suggested that if we don't die there won't be room for others to have a chance of having this earthly experience. Zach asked, "Would anyone want to live on earth forever?"

Cynthia didn't want to be talked out of her fear, "It doesn't make any kind of sense that our whole lives, no matter what is going on, the truth is we are always one day closer to our own death. We live to die."

It was good to be working on a project so the conversation need not flow steadily. Talking gaps and spaces were natural and normal as they dealt with the job at hand. Cynthia continued, "Life and death are intertwined, actually, both are real. They go together. And no wonder improvements to life on earth happen slowly, because death takes away someone like Francine who has wisdom to offer others." Justin remembered the Francine folders Sherry shared with him on her beachside balcony.

Zach proposed the next generation brings new ways of solving problems, making improvements, "If the first generation that ever was still is all there is, how stagnant, stale, stymying that might be. Perhaps Life is wanting to unveil itself by bringing in new people, phasing out those who have made their contributions, or not. Of course, there is DNA, so maybe all generations are ever with us."

Cynthia was intrigued with Zach's comment about Life wanting to unveil Itself. She compared his vocabulary with her revolutionary preferences, "Life wanting to unveil Itself resonates more with me than saying God wants to unveil, reveal Himself. Along with Dee's suggestion that Christianity as myth needs restoration, or evolving replenishment. I say restorations happen with a new way of speaking. Instead of saying 'thank God,' we might instead say 'thank heaven(s).' The term 'Higher Power' seems more agreeable these days than 'God.' The Holy Spirit might become Creative Spirit; speak of Jesus as the Cosmic Christ. Use the word 'transition' instead of the words, *death, dying*. Tie myth to mystery; the

Grand Mystery Life Is." Zach asked whether someone murdered, killed, would be said to have transitioned? Cynthia was pleased her captive audience of two workmen assembling the quirky curio dutifully dealt with their task while she talked. She'd pondered the Resurrection paintings in the book she'd given Dee for Easter. She read enough of the book to feel it presented Easter as the realization, the awareness of universal resurrection for everyone, rather than celebrating the individual resurrection of Jesus alone.

Just then, Pixie-Pickett wanted to go outside. Cynthia took her outdoors for a short doggie toilet visit where, as often before, Cynthia wondered who and where was the genius who thought to put hand inside plastic bag, pick-up doggie-droppings, invert bag, tie shut, in a simple sanitary operation. The first person who did that was brilliant, Cynthia chuckled to herself.

Back inside the house, Cynthia heard Justin say, "My father's suicide casts a peculiar shadow on death for me. I am unable to process death without also dealing with his desperation of not wanting to live. You didn't know my dad well, did you?"

"I did not," Zach confirmed.

Justin related, "The idea of universal resurrection has great appeal for me because of my dad's suicide. I want him to be healed of his inability to enjoy being alive, not wanting to live. I don't think so much in terms of his need to be "forgiven," but rather his need for "healing," which I find far more agreeable, and more likely."

Cynthia casually commented, "I understand the Catholic tradition of ashes on the forehead on Ash Wednesday. At least once a year everyone should remember the inevitability of death," tenderly placing her hand on Justin's shoulder as he sat on the floor assembling the curio. He momentarily put his hand over hers.

These newlyweds each had the tragic death of a parent as part of their individual stories: Cynthia's biological mother Roxanne, and Justine's father Henri. Then, too, Cynthia never forgot she thought her father was dying when he had his panic attack. Some memories do not fade.

CHAPTER FORTY

Oriana Moving Back to Town

Something wonderful came to be. Dee's sidewalk professor friend Oriana, after spending a Covid-quarantine winter in New York state with relatives following her husband's death, decided to move back to Sandshell, to warmer weather. She stayed with Dee and Zach while she looked for a condo to buy, and then again while waiting for her furniture to arrive. It felt to Dee as if the huge hole left by Francine's death was not now quite as overwhelming with Oriana in town.

Oriana was an animated conversationalist whose black eyes danced with excitement when engaged in a topic of interest. Her salt and pepper uncontrollable curly hair seemed exceptionally alive when dealing with ideas. Oriana exuded energy. She was presently intent on understanding the large number of people attracted to Qanon on the internet. She shared Dee's concern of why the word myth has come to mean falsehood, and aware that fewer people identify themselves with the Judeo-Christian myth, at least not in a formal way, according to polls.

As Oriana, Dee and Zach were on the patio after the evening meal, Oriana was saying she felt it fair to consider the Judeo-Christian myth the dominant myth of this country where still, even today, Santa Claus and the Easter Bunny are well-known; at the inauguration of a new president he places his hand on the bible to take the oath of office. People in a court case swear to tell the truth, the whole truth, "so help me God." We sing God bless America, and the Battle Hymn of the Republic. In the pledge of allegiance, the words "one nation under God" are said. On our paper money are printed the words, "In God We Trust."

Zach asked, "What about the concept of freedom. Is this part of the American myth?" He already knew the answer, for he and Dee had talked about this. As important as freedom is in this country, freedoms of all sorts, including freedom of religion, are advocated. However, the idea of freedom is not big enough to qualify as myth. Myth is cosmological. Myth is about life, death, and everything in-between, such as why being alive involves struggle, suffering, the whole human condition, its purpose or meaninglessness, its perversity and preciousness. Myth is the biggest story possible with ultimate questions and answers.

Dee wondered aloud, "If the Judeo-Christian myth is fading, why? Perhaps the people in the pews are spoiled children, fickle, willful, full of themselves. Or, the clerics have too little wisdom, too little inspiration for the flock." She already had temporary answers to her question but wanted to hear more from Zach and Oriana.

Oriana remained impressed with what Dee had done with Jesus' parables, and shared Dee's interest in hermeneutics (interpretation), and translation. She said, "During the Covid pandemic I've almost daily participated in TV Masses, listened to many sermons. Having been a teacher, I know it is impossible to be consistently profound. I appreciate that the Eucharist is life-giving even when the homily is uninspiring, however, I become more alive when a sermon is alive with interpretive insights; when metaphoric and symbolic understanding is plucked from the readings.

"As Dee's fourfold treatment of Jesus' parables shows, there is pertinent psychological material to be discerned. Without symbol and metaphor, the material can remain bland, with too many sermons mere versions of what one has heard again and again without significant impact; not hitting home."

Dee understood, "I heard a sermon on there being two creation stories in Jewish scripture in the book of Genesis, and in Christian scripture two Christmas stories; one in the gospel of Matthew, and the other in Luke. The versions are quite different from each other, which shows various accounts, multiple sources, which together expand meaning, perspective. Somewhat like witnesses in a court case whose testimonies need not be identical to inform.

"Hearing about these duplicate bible stories I began searching on my own and stumbled on a goldmine in a book on androgyny which helped me understand today's gender confusion." Dee did not mention her own earlier gender troubles.

Dee left the table briefly to return with the androgyny book, citing specific page numbers (pp. 63-65) from which she read, "In the first creation story in Genesis it is written that on the sixth day of creation God said:

"*Let us* make man in *our image, after our likeness*; and let *them* have dominion over the fish of the sea . . . and over all the earth, and over every creeping thing that creeps upon the earth." So God created man in his own image, in the image of God he created him; *male and female* he created *them*. And God blessed *them* and God said to *them*, "Be fruitful and multiply, and fill the earth and subdue it . . ." (Genesis 1:26-28)

Dee elaborated with fervor about feminine-masculine throughout creation, including the Godhead. The animal world is made of masculine-feminine, as are some plants, and, of course, humans, said in the above quote to be made in the image of God. She read commentaries on the bible passage, and realized she returned to this Genesis verse repeatedly because it was so important to her.

"She returned also to the 2000 book, *Androgyny: the opposites within* by June Singer, psychotherapist trained in the depth psychology of Carl Jung, and noted from the back cover of the book, important statements,

"Consciousness of our own androgyny can lead to a new sense of personal unity within the larger universe. It is no accident that men and women today are expressing previously undeveloped sides of their natures . . . Masculine/feminine interaction within each of us is not only normal but the dynamic factor in our wholeness."

Dee added, "I'm not sure we are today understanding our own androgyny with much depth, much meaningful insight. We have piecemeal notions that surgeries and hormone injections can change our bodies and we've fixed a problem, yet we cannot change whatever the soul is, which seems to be androgynous. We need to sit with this conundrum longer than we have to understand what is going on with gender issues."

Dee explained, as she had to others, "In the depth psychology of Carl Jung, he names the feminine energy in a male, *anima*—and the masculine energy in a woman, *animus*. June Singer describes androgyny as opposite, complementary, contradictory. Whereas, in Iain McGilchrist's brain-hemisphere book *The Master and His Emissary*, he says the two sides of the brain compete. He also says the brain hemispheres inhibit each other. They work together. Their differences are needed for survival.

"McGilchrist does not deal with androgyny in his book. However, Singer's book includes split-brain research (pp. 156-159), which reinforces what Francine taught using a Mobius band about masculine and feminine energies."

Dee concluded, "Singer's book on androgyny may still be ahead of its time. The first edition came out in 1976, then 1989, and again in 2000, four years before she died. It takes several generations for some ideas to be widely understood in the culture-at-large, and I believe androgyny may be a slow-to-understand topic."

The gender turmoil Dee experienced continued to be healed by helpful information in books, podcasts and such. She remained convinced that the present practice of medical procedures altering the body was beside the point—that psychological complementarity within humans was mistakenly being treated as physical malady, so far as Dee could determine, while she was always willing to learn.

Oriana, a good listener as well as a treasure-trove of replenishing ideas, was happily back in Sandshell. Dee was eager for her to become part of the Brunch Bunch, though it was immediately obvious this wasn't going to be as easy as Dee had expected.

CHAPTER FORTY-ONE

Lunch in the Clarksdale Park

Mid-July, with Covid-vaccinations readily available throughout the country, Zach and Dee drove to Clarksdale KS, to be with Charles, pregnant Kendal, grandson Monty—Julia and Marc, Monty's other grandparents. Monty, an ambitious toddler was amusing to behold, and his parents seemed to be thriving.

The days in Clarksdale passed pleasantly and quickly. Zach and Marc spent hours on the golf course, while Julia and Dee talked hours away. One evening meal included Kendal's brother Patrick, wife Brooke, and young toddler Matti. After the isolation of Covid-quarantine, this inclusive family gathering was ever so satisfying.

Masks continued to be worn by the employees at Montel Furniture. The sheer number of customers made that seem wise, for the store was flooded with customers now that Covid-vaccinations were becoming widespread. Unfortunately, the aggressive Delta variant of Covid was on the rise.

Charles lunched at a downtown restaurant with his dad-Zach and mum-Dee. He'd become even more handsomely mature, hardworking, responsible, with his steadfast humor remaining. Conversation with

Charles was a joy, so that another noon, the three ordered take-out from a downtown restaurant, drove to the town's spacious park, where they found a table and felt free to converse without ears close to them, as would have been the case in the restaurant. Seated outdoors with privacy their conversation became what each had learned because of the pandemic.

Charles said he came to appreciate the financial savvy of Kendal's dad at the furniture store who had, over the years, invested money wisely and thus been able to keep the business afloat, his employees paid, during this unpredictable time.

Zach said he had renewed admiration in humans from the kindness and dedication he saw in volunteers in food banks, and in medical personnel with their care-giving generosity, sometimes risking their own lives, and what he saw in neighbors helping neighbors, in which he included Dee's vegetable garden.

Dee said the mystery of life had deepened for her. Why are there viruses? Why was this pandemic politically polarized? Why had internet Qanon found an audience? Why the insurrection on the U.S. Capitol on January 6? Overall, she was investigating the word myth, which had come to mean falsehood. Myth as falsehood became the enduring topic of their lunch.

She told of this book Francine had given her. *The Freedom of Man in Myth*. The Greek meaning of *mythos* simply means speech, word, story. How does this relate to freedom? Freedom from what? Dee had her own version of the relationship between myth and freedom.

"As you know, I believe Western Culture has brilliantly developed left-hemisphere brain talents leaving right-hemisphere approaches behind, and even more importantly, the dance between the hemispheres unclear, which has taken a toll on hermeneutic freedom—how we interpret our experiences. On one hand we think, think, think about what we experience. We take a rational approach. However, we can also rationalize, conflate, subvert, sabotage logic. On the other hand, we practice science, collect data, do research. However, not all of life can be stuffed into the scientific paradigm. Life and experience are bigger than rationality or science."

Charles leap-frogged into an example, "If I wanted to collect data on who I should marry, I would need to marry different women, live with each, have children with each, collect the compatibility data, and then make my choice. Polygamy is a version of this. Or simply serial living together, skipping the marriage part.

Zach added, "Just as human experience is greater than rationality or science, I say God is more than religion; greater than the religious impulse in humans. Neither science or rationality is sufficient to contain or explain religion, and certainly not capable of containing God which is beyond comprehension. So, in a sense, we today might be limited, entrapped in science and a rational approach to God, which is an inadequate hermeneutic habit, to use Dee's words."

Dee smiled agreeably, "Yes. Myth is where the biggest questions, the seemingly unanswerable questions live. Neither science or rationality, or the both of them together, can satisfy the biggest questions. Myth can at least contain the questions even if it doesn't have all the answers."

Charles spoke haltingly, "I've thought about rationality and Nazi concentration camps. There is a certain demented logic to kill those deemed unfit to live. Why not kill those declared vermin? Those labeled unacceptable, however insane, destructive, evil that judgment. Then, efficiently and effectively obliterate the likes of them and build a society of superlative people, the Aryan race. Isn't there some kind of sick-logic about such a conclusion?

Zach reacted, "Very, very sick, indeed."

Dee responded, "That's why the fourfold format I used with Jesus' parables, which includes the "moral sense" is so necessary—alongside the psychological sense, which can cause personalities to wonder about themselves, personal choices, convictions, courage, cowardice."

Dee confided that lunch in the park, "I presently see resistance in Monique about accepting Oriana wholeheartedly. Monique feels accepting Oriana into the Brunch Bunch is betraying Francine. She has said it is like Henri marrying "new wife" the day after their divorce was final. No respect for anybody, anything."

Francine, as French-speaking Canadian and real-estate client was, in a special way for Monique, her exclusive friend. Only days ago, Monique told Dee her reaction to Oriana may be due to lingering powerlessness, which still has her in its grip, "Sometimes I need too much outer control, when mostly I actually need control with feelings, my own feelings," Monique critiqued herself.

The park-lunch in Clarksdale with Charles and his parents continued with more talk of freedom and unfreedom, and how the Judeo-Christian historical-myth has neither the precision of science nor the consistency or clarity of rationality, but is known to bring hope to humanity, when understood and practiced at its best.

Charles summarized, "A lot of life is non-provable and non-rational."

Zach eerily reflected, "I'd say my panic attack came from other than my rational capacities. It seemed to come out of nowhere. Today it doesn't seem real, though the memory of the attack stirs fear inside me. I'd say it was raw fear unleashed in my body—possibly triggered by my thoughts, my rationality. I have only you two and Cynthia to confirm what happened—and hospital records, perhaps, but the attack was over before I got to the hospital. I don't know why I bring this up, but it was so real I don't want to forget what happened. Somehow it seems to fit with what we're talking about.

"To a large degree we are what and how we interpret," Dee observed, and consistently maintained. "I desperately wonder whether Christianity at this time in history needs to reinterpret the nature of God as masculine and feminine, recorded in Genesis 1:26-28, thus correcting the assumption of earthlings that God is merely male. Now that brain-hemisphere difference has been uncovered, might we infer that being made in the image of God as male and female—that the Life Source can be thought of as both feminine-masculine energy? Dee knew her words were simplistic, perhaps even beside the point. Yet this Genesis probability did not go away.

CHAPTER FORTY-TWO

Myth Helps Us Rise Above

Shortly after Francine's death, Sherry had invited Dee to Francine's library whereupon Dee borrowed several books, and began reading, *Tracking the Gods: The Place of Myth in Modern Life*, (1995) by well-known psychotherapist, depth-psychologist, Jungian analyst, James Hollis. As she read, she thought to herself, *This book was published twenty-six years ago—before our nation became massively opioid-addicted or as politically-polarized as we are today.* She summarized in her own words what stuck in her mind from this little book on myth:

> The more a culture loses its mythic ties, the more prone it is to substance abuse . . . today, many remain psychologically infantile, narcissistically preoccupied, avoiding pain and responsibility, looking for a magical person who will make life meaningful and painless, while they themselves pretend immortality. . . there is the lure of group-think; looking for easy answers in a group or Great Leader.[18]

---

[18] James Hollis, *Tracking the Gods: The Place of Myth in Modern Life*, (1995), pp. 113- 114.

Dee was most impressed with the idea of pretending immortality. What are the consequences of pretending immortality? She repeated to herself, *If I were to ignore the reality that I am going to die someday.*

She condensed more that Hollis wrote,

> Some political radicals are terrified by ambiguity, self-examination and cultural diversity. Beneath this is fanaticism and fearfulness . . . Other political radicals delight in secularism, think they can live without god, disdain theological reflection. They tend to be driven by anger.[19]

And so, Hollis saw political extremes as driven by fear and anger. Dee again saw Zach's wisdom using the image of the human eye to illustrate people stuck politically, able only to look out of a corner of the eye, limited by a lens of fear or anger, whereas in the spacious center of the eye a broad political spectrum is possible, a wide horizon, the freedom of creative possibility. Moderate, centered politics is not one point, but a spectrum, a range of observation, opinion, decision, belief. And where does myth fit into this? The question about myth was never far from Dee these days.

Dee remembered Francine's book, *The Freedom of Man in Myth* (1968) with its revealing title: myth brings to humankind a certain kind of freedom. Myth is a repository of infinite speculation. Yes, including speculation about Infinite, Eternal reality, possibility. Written by Kees W. Bolle (1927-2012), a Dutch historian, professor of History of Religions at UCLA, whose main interest was Indian religions. Dee summarized pithy phrases gleaned from the book:

> Myth restores the freedom to live in the world as it is . . . myth's power is to liberate humans from everyday, exhausting, common experience (p. 86) . . . myth helps us rise above the tension of the opposites (p. 87) . . . myth destroys the oppressive finiteness of humanity (p. 88) . . . Myth does not deal with trifles (p. 49) . . . myth is not an idle rhapsody, not an aimless outpouring of vain imaginings (p. 50) . . . myth is not a theory. It is first and foremost

---

[19] Hollis, *Tracking the Gods,* p. 98.

something that happens; it is *recited, chanted, enacted* (p. 84) . . . myth bears on philosophy, psychology, sociology, cultural anthropology, and many another academic specialization . . . but none of these specializations can deal with myth exhaustively (p. 87).[20]

Dee knew *mythos* in Greek means story, word, speech. Myth typically has to do with stories about ultimate, crucial, perplexing mystery: creation, living, struggling, suffering, dying. Myth happens outside controlled variables or systematic thought, or precise clarity. Myth includes inspiration, insight, religious impulse, and yes, humor. Dee, Zach and Charles talked about hermeneutic freedom in myth, and our cultural hermeneutic poverty today.

The three wondered whether Qanon is an internet gimmick which found a myth-starved audience from those in literalized fear-based Christianity, or as fallout from those disappointed, disenchanted with time-worn Christianity that has not been sufficiently open to renewal, though Vatican II advocated such. These and similar questions did not let go. The three having lunch in a park in Clarksdale KS were compelled to continue wondering.

---

[20] Kees W. Bolle, *The Freedom of Man in Myth* (1968).

CHAPTER FORTY-THREE

Humorous Monty

During Zach and Dee's stay in Clarksdale KS with Charles and family, Kendal as mother and mother-to-be, wife, lawyer, worked mostly from home during the Covid-quarantine, with grandmother Julia helping out with toddler Monty, while babysitter-housekeeper Consuela was furloughed with pay, just as Charles and Kendal were paid during the winter Covid-quarantine, and felt Consuela's continuing wage only fair. Now, vaccinated, mask-wearing Consuela was back at work in the house. Why was mask-wearing controversial, politicized?

Dee thought of the fear-anger dynamics in political extremes. She thought also of the same dynamics in Catholicism at the present time for and against Pope Francis. It was Kendal at an evening meal who raised the topic of the current controversy over Pope Francis's decision to limit celebrating Mass in Latin thus increasing the more widespread practice of celebrating the 1970 Mass which follows the guidelines of Vatican II.

Kendal asked Dee, "Do you suppose fear and anger are at the root of the heated reactions on this topic? Does God care whether Latin or English, or whatever language is used?" Dee laughed and thoughtfully responded, "Well I don't know God's concerns. It's human reaction and reasoning we're dealing with. Each language is its own kind of carrier, revealer, designator. As a child, I attended Mass celebrated in Latin, but felt no pangs when it changed to English. I love the openness of Vatican II. Some greatly fear change.

"I was in great need of soul-healing. That was always what I was looking for, whether or not I was consciously aware of that. The part of the Mass that still speaks most directly to me are the words, 'Only say the word and my soul will be healed.'" Kendal and Charles may have felt Dee was simply being down-to-earth, knowing nothing of the gender dilemma she lived with for years.

Dee related, "Through my own experience, I've always assumed all people had parts of their personality they wanted healed. Maybe many people do not know they need healing—need to be graced into fullness. Healing in general is, of course, a huge part of the story of Jesus, the cosmic pathfinder. It's sometimes easier to confirm physical healing which is more obvious to observe, however inner healing, healing of psyche (soul), may often be part of physical healing."

To Dee it seemed, "Jesus, gifting humanity with the simple act of sharing bread and wine, whether elaborated in Latin or one's own language, puts one in a dimension of healing reality where maladies of all sorts are touched; made better. Perhaps the familiarity of Latin to some is precious; the mystery of a dead language, adding to the mystery of the Mass.

"Some hold onto tradition out of fear that change will cause chaos and collapse. Some agitate for change, angry that change doesn't happen fast enough. Pope Francis is the target at the center of the pushes and pulls of fear and anger. Like Zach's analogy of the human eye, I see Pope Francis in an arena of wide-range vision, inviting many perspectives, bombarded on all sides, but in the end he must decide. His is not an easy job.

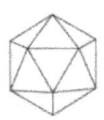 "In his encyclical *Fratelli Tutti* the Pope promotes copious dialogue, analogous to a polyhedron," which Zach drew on his napkin, a family tradition begun by Francine drawing on napkins at patio dinners that special summer.

Kendal was a careful listener, "I've never before heard Jesus referred to as a cosmic pathfinder." Dee laughed, "I enjoy new ways of labeling him. I believe he inaugurated an energy field, which we call the Holy Spirit, that is available to earthlings. His personality, the era in which he lived, people around him at that time, and later St. Paul, declared him Messiah Jesus."

Kendal questioned, "But what about suffering? The Messiah did not make all that go away." Dee gave an answer she and Sherry talked about on occasion, "Ultimately, the Totality of Life, in order to be Total, is made up of all possibilities—everything has its opposite, everything creative has an opposite destructive side, and what is destructive may have some creative aspects.

"It makes sense to me that the creative obviously outweighs the destructive or everybody and everything would long ago have vanished, been annihilated. Human choices augment or diminish what is creative, what is destructive, or there is often a mix of the two."

Charles lightheartedly contributed, "This might be an example: There are countless blessings living with Kendal, Monty, in this place, but there is the curse of no beach." He bowed his head in humor as if crushed by not living near a beach. Just then, Monty in his high-chair banged his hand down into his food splattering it about. Perfect timing. Peals of laughter, including from the young one, mimicking the adults in laughter after first gasping, startling himself as food hit his face. Monty's hand banging coincided with Charles's words and head bowing.

Why was this humorous? It's hard to say. Humor connected to unacceptable behavior; creating a mess that had to be cleaned-up. Laughing at behavior adults don't want reinforced, thus repeated. Childish impulse creating comedy and a bother at the same time; adults left with the dilemma of indicating disapproval while obviously amused; a mix of everyday ambiguity, paradox, synchronicity?

Zach, Dee, and now Kendal and Charles who'd been introduced to the notion of "myth" since the arrival of Dee and Zach, as the overwhelmingly large chunk of life that fits into neither science or reason, were thinking about whether myth was involved.

Cleaning up spattered food, Kendal observed, "If you told someone the story of this happening, it would never be as funny as it was to us. Re-telling the story, one might need to add, the phrase, 'You had to be there.' The stories I hear in law cases are like that. Most of life is like this, neither science or logic, but many-sided, with various mythical perspectives that don't add-up to either falsehood, as is now done with the word *myth*, nor is stark truth always at stake. Scientific-rationality can only add up to an inadequate hermeneutic, impoverished understanding."

Dee added, "Which is why literal reading of the bible tends to be short-sighted. One needs to look around corners, ask questions, wonder. Why was this Monty-incident funny? When I re-create mental images of what happened, it's still funny to me."

Charles, cleaning up Monty while Kendal wiped the surroundings, suggested, "It might have been annoying, only and completely annoying, and not the least humorous, yet it's humorous."

Zach had the answer, "Any worthwhile comedian knows it's all in the timing, right, Monty?"

Monty's mood had turned sour. He wanted to be back in his high-chair, eating. First, he was startled by what he'd done, which took his breath away. Then, he laughed with the others. Now, he was irritated that food-getting had been interrupted.

Kendal thought aloud as she finished cleaning the area. "Humor defies scientific-rationality; humor is outside their boundaries. Do animals have a sense of humor, comedic ability? Monty can be funny when he wants to be, although I don't believe he was trying to be funny just now."

The meal continued without incident. It's true, humor is neither scientific or logical, but indeed, refreshing.

CHAPTER FORTY-FOUR

Julia, No Longer Angry

Next day, Dee and Julia spent together at Julia's house while caring for young Monty and his younger cousin Matti, giving their mothers a day-out; cousins together without parents. Grandmothers Dee and Julia enjoying their time together while contributing to a day of freedom for the young mothers, while Zach and Charles were on the golf course.

Dee and Zach liked the town of Clarksdale, with extended family, though indeed without a beach, but with a most unusual octagonal house, its own glass hut in the backyard, and the boundless Kansas sky.

Dee shared with Julia the story of Monty's timely food splash at last night's dinner table. Julia appreciated the incident. Dee mentioned her interest in myth as encompassing much life-experience, including humor, which is not in the category of scientific-rationalism, and how equating myth with falsehood is so very wrong.

Dee added predictably, "Perhaps people starved for myth, which is beyond scientific-rationalism, are today's Qanon audience, hooked by vague, mythical-seeming statements of Qanon—drenched in falseness itself." Dee immediately realized Julia didn't comprehend what she'd just said about myth and falseness, as if Dee plucked verbiage out of nowhere, with no background, no context in which Julia could make sense of it.

Julia realized this, too, "Ann Dramm told me she hoped one day the two of us, you and me, would meet, as she felt you were an idea-person like my biological mother, Matti." Julia's voice slightly faltered with emotion mentioning the original Matti. "And then, we did meet at Ann's funeral. Life has its ways with us, which at this moment seems most fortunate, though we can be slammed by life as well."

Yes, Dee recognized herself an idea-person as she grew older—thus ever so pleased Oriana was again living in Sandshell. In Dee's present obsession with recovering myth from falsehood, she remembered an evening months before the Covid quarantine, before Cynthia and Sherry exchanged Quinn and Justin, when Cynthia, abuzz with energy after being with Sherry when they chuckled about more than inch-long German words. The two German words distinguished between different kinds of inquiry and knowing. Both are labeled *Wissenschaften* (sciences) in German. *Naturwissenschaften* (natural sciences) do research, gather data, use mathematics, can replicate and predict. The other kind of inquiry and knowing is *Geisteswissenschaften* (sciences of the spirit): history, literature, philosophy, theology, fine arts, and so on.

Cynthia's brief comments that evening ignited Dee's interest, who'd learned enough about herself to recognize when something made her feel energized. Thus, she began learning more about Cynthia's long German words and came to know the German philosopher Wilhelm Windelband (1848-1915) explained fundamental differences between these two approaches to knowledge.

Windelband labeled *Naturwissenschaften* (natural sciences) nomothetic, searching for general laws, using mathematics, able to replicate situations—make predictions. *Geisteswissenschaften* (sciences of the spirit) are concerned not with general laws, but with single events that will not happen again, which Dee understood Greek philosopher Heraclitus (544 b.c.e. - 485 b.c.e.) meant when he said "No man ever steps in the same river twice, for it's not the same river and he's not the same man."

Julia retrieved something she and Dee had talked about in the past, "Heraclitus was correct. Change is constant. Everything changes except change itself. My feelings about birth mother Matti have changed over the years. I'm no longer angry with her for giving me away. She might not have been a capable mother and knew it. She obviously didn't want Cal involved. She did the right thing, allowing me to have my parents as my parents. I'm now grateful she gave me away, though the words 'gave me away' still smacks of an act I cannot fathom. I have purposely come to say the words 'she gave me away' so as to desensitize me to those words as they become more and more commonplace to me, thus losing their sting one utterance at a time.

"Cal remains in my life. He's remarried, you know; always remembers my birthday and I e-mail occasionally, updating him on family happenings. I've forgiven Matti for never contacting him about the pregnancy and my birth. A part of me admires her independent spirit, taking it upon herself to handle the situation herself.

"I'm ever-grateful to have known Ann Dramm, and Beth, remaining members of the Texas Trio. For me, ancient Greek philosopher Heraclitus was right about not being able to step into the same river twice, for it's not the same river and the person is not the same person.

"Again and again, I prayed, 'Please, God, I want to stop being angry,' as I stepped into my own angry river about having been given away by Matti, slowly learning to pray for Matti—that she could forgive herself, for Ann Dramm told me Matti carried the sorrow of giving me away to the grave. In addition, I more avidly prayed prayers of gratitude for my parents who raised me, and finally I was surprisingly able to encourage Patrick and Brooke wanting to name their baby girl Matti, and now that name carries joy for me. I do not live in the past, but in the goodness of now."

The days in Clarksdale passed quickly for Dee and Zach. And then, back home in Sandshell, Julia's comment about living in the 'goodness of now' would gain in importance for Dee.

CHAPTER FORTY-FIVE

Change, Blowing in the Wind

In Sandshell, Cynthia, Justin, and Pixie-Pickett were doing well. Oriana was into trying to understand the current Latin Mass controversy. Monique was busy with the hot real-estate market and Christiane's wedding; too busy to remain disappointed that Sherry decided to buy Francine's condo, which meant Monique couldn't purchase it. Monique knew she would miss Christiane and Jameson living with her. She dreaded their departure from her house.

Estelle's life turned a corner when she met Feldon, a silver-haired African-American male walking a dog while she was walking Angus, the dog of son Lee's family, out of town on a short vacation. Estelle was house-sitting, dog-sitting. Upon this early morning meeting, animated, extraverted, good-enough-looking Feldon Sprague introduced himself, and after talking fifteen minutes or so, she gave indications of walking on, he scribbled his e-mail address on a piece of paper, which he tore off and handed to her. They talked a bit more. She told him her husband of fifty-five years died a year and a half ago; that they had three sons, that she'd been a high school counselor. It was unlike Estelle to share so much so quickly.

She was flattered by Feldon's attention, curious about him, cautious, uncertain. She found him fascinating. His e-mail address included his first and last name, which she looked up on the internet. He was a lawyer in town. He'd told her he was mostly retired in Florida, divorced, originally from New Hampshire, appeared reputable per the internet.

The next morning, and the next, Estelle walked Angus on different routes. It was up to her to decide whether she would send an e-mail to Feldon, which seemed a safe thing to do. Estelle had begun to recognize loneliness in herself. When Reggie died, there was shock and sorrow, mixed with relief from the difficulties of dealing with his dementia. Now, a year and a half later, a time when Covid-19 continued to dominate the headlines, Estelle found herself not exactly drowning in loneliness, but somewhat in its clutches.

She was grateful for her friendships in the Brunch Bunch and with familiar female colleagues from the high school where she'd been a counselor, but she yearned for masculine energy. This came as a surprise to her. Some might say she was a sex-starved widow, but they'd be wrong. She desired not the complications of a sexual relationship, but the conversation of a male—the friendship of a male. She missed Reggie, his masculine energy, which had often driven her crazy.

She had enjoyed talking with Feldon that one time, though he did most of the talking. She told no one of this specific kind of loneliness she was experiencing. Son Lee and family returned home and Estelle went back to her own home with Feldon's e-mail address. Would she contact him? She could at least say she'd enjoyed their conversation.

After several days in her own home, she sent an e-mail, "Enjoyed the conversation." She purposely did not say, "Enjoyed *our* conversation," to avoid any hint of familiarity." Feldon promptly e-mailed back, and thus began short e-mails, back and forth. Estelle told no one.

Meanwhile, romance was desperately trying to find a way to marriage between Sherry and Quinn. They set a date for their wedding after torturously working through that, which at times, seemed questions without answers, insurmountable obstacles to their marriage. At the same time, Quinn carefully followed the Latin Mass controversy these late summer days after Pope Francis in an official letter in July put restraints on the celebration of the Latin Mass.

Oriana, too, followed the Latin Mass issue and confided to Dee, "Catholics adamantly for the Latin Mass seem to believe that church pews and seminaries will be overflowing if only Pope Francis encouraged the Latin Mass rather than limiting it from becoming more common-place. These "traditionalists" seem to find something magical about go-ing back to medieval beliefs, practices, attitudes.

"I grew-up with the Latin Mass, the priest's back to the congregation, women's hair covered with hat or veil. I find today's modernized Mass which formed out of the sessions and documents of Vatican II refresh-ing, liberating, uplifting, with the Eucharist celebrated in the language of each specific country, priest facing the people.

"I remain fond of pope John XXIII, responsible for calling Vatican II, opening the Council in 1962 with a marvelous metaphor, "open the windows and let in the fresh air." I remember my optimism; there would be married clergy, women priests. I remember the hopefulness I felt when I heard from Vatican II the phrase, 'the Church is the People of God.' However, more than fifty years later, Pope Francis is still struggling to let in fresh air, while "traditionalists" want to go to a past where I felt there was a lot of stale air, stifling and suffocating, defensive and inflexi-ble.

"Latin Mass traditionalists want to go back in time, though I some-times wonder whether they appreciate the fact that over 2,000 bishops took part took part in Vatican II, voted on specific topics. The docu-ments coming out of Vatican II didn't reflect the discernment of just a few people.

"I see this impulse in backward-looking countries with a strong im-pulse for men to control women. Is there so much fear of women's in-dependence, that only by living in the past when women were under the thumb of men, the males feel sure of their own power?

"I've heard it said men tend to be unaware of their own sadness; that men often are afraid of other men, which I guess, goes hand-in-hand with fierce male competition. Some males are perhaps entrapped in too small a part of themselves, and need liberation into their fuller being, their inner depths.

"I believe the struggles of Covid have only exacerbated the intense cultural struggles which began in this country in the 1960s, including

Vatican II (1962-1965). The fallout of the Council has been ongoing since then. Some Catholics want to live pre-Vatican II. "When will the struggle end?" asked Oriana, and answered her own question with musical levity. "The answer, my friend, is blowing in the wind. The answer is blowing in the wind," lyrics of a song from the sixties. Dee appreciated Oriana's lighthearted answer, accompanied by Oriana's hand gesture of throwing her hands up as if blowing in the wind. Oriana was almost as animated as Monique.

Dee summarized, "The winds of change can be hard to navigate," and using Zach's eye analogy, "Fearful people looking out of a corner of the eye want to backpedal, are stuck in what philosopher Paul Ricoeur labeled a hermeneutic of suspicion, whereas angry people looking out of the other corner of the eye, advocate radical reckless change at breakneck speed. They also are stuck in a hermeneutic of suspicion, with never-ending deconstruction of culture. While the large area in the center of the eye symbolizes healthy, complex conversation, dialogue, mature religious understanding, re-thinking situations, bringing forth subtlety and nuance, discernment rather than knee-jerk reaction, the ability to deal with the tension of the opposites, a hermeneutic of trusting hope. I believe this is what Pope Francis expresses using the image of the geometric polyhedron."

Oriana's quick mind added, "And Pope Francis uses the format of a synod, which is a meeting, an assembly or limited council in a church to gather viewpoints, thrash about specific issues regarding doctrine, administration or implementation of policy. Synods can produce a plethora of perspectives on a particular topic(s). Protestant churches also use synods.

"My opinion is that Pope Francis values an abundance of viewpoints that come forth in a synod. As a Jesuit trained in seeking divine illumination or guidance, the art of discernment, Pope Francis is able to hold an "overflow"" of polarities, some might say, allowing the Holy Spirit, to create a new way of seeing in humans; a situation which transcends the opposites, the polarities."

Oriana continued, "In the classroom I've seen this with students, some angry with extreme reactions, others fearfully reactionary, still others less radical; more stable and secure. When I had the courage and confidence to let this clashing happen in a class, there could emerge an

exchange of ideas, breakthrough understanding, potential partial recon-
ciliations, more compassionate, empathetic dynamics at play, instead of
flinging impassioned platitudes at each other. Dee knew impassioned
flingings herself.

CHAPTER FORTY-SIX

Cynthia, Taming Her Tongue

Dee had lived in pockets of fearful defiant anger before moving to Stamford, where, positively influenced by aunt Tess, then lovingly nursing her aunt until she died in Florida, where Dee met Charles, Cynthia, and Mrs. Arndt, and then Zach. Looking back over her own life, Dee found she disagreed somewhat with Francine's guarded view of romantic love, though she agreed romantic attraction that does not mature into genuinely loving another, may not endure the knottiness (naughtiness, she amused herself with same sound, drastically different spelling and meaning of knottiness/naughtiness)—of everyday existence.

Dee was amused by words, sentences. For instance, she realized the difference a miniscule change in wording can make. For instance: "with little assistance" compared to "with **a** little assistance." "With little assistance" suggests sole effort. "With **a** little assistance" emphasizes help received.

She thought of the power of a comma: **Please God**, exhorting, commanding one to, appease, impress—compared to **Please, God**, which seems a prayer for help. Dee's respect for words was upset with today's interpretation of **myth** as **falsehood**. She and Oriana talked about today's crippled hermeneutic; about the problem of Christian myth having stagnated. They talked about humanities helping humans relate to their own daily experience through the experiences, depictions of others in art, music, poetry, stories, myths, history, and not merely fed piecemeal by scientific fact(s). Myth, soul, humanities go together, they decided.

Oriana drew a spiral. The spiral represents growth in human under-standing, a progressively higher-broader-deeper view, perspective, about living and inevitably dying. Throughout a lifetime, this seems to be the path we're on. Not a straight line, Myth is paradoxical, ambig-uous, plausible rather than factual. Myth  is story; not merely fact-based story, though myth may include or allude to facts of recorded history.

Myth is story that emerges out of the whole of human experience, human imagination, inspiration, tradition; including metaphor and sym-bol. Myth certainly is not pure falsehood. Religion is neither science or strict rationality. Religion at its core is myth that can be interpreted in wholesome ways or in chronically constricted, fearful, angry, controlling ways.

Oriana and Dee concluded all experience is from within, and includes intuition, discernment, discretion, deepest longings, consciousness, awareness itself. They underlined the word "Human" in Humanities.

Days later, Cynthia spent time with Dee, talking about books she'd been reading during the summer between making plans for a second-grade class in a real room in the Fall. She read a book that speaks about freedom, not political freedom, but intimate personal freedom. In this book, a character questions how free each of us actually is, by talking about factors that limit personal freedom: genetics, specific DNA, meta-bolic uniqueness, morphic resonance, morphogenetic fields (generational stuff which can be both positive and negative), social influences, acquired habits creating synaptic bonds and pathways in your brain, plus advertis-ing, propaganda, countless paradigms influencing a person.

Cynthia tied this view of limited freedom to today's opioid crisis, which for some reason had been her concern since the early days of Covid. She had this vivid impression that once Covid was under control, the opioid crisis would still be rampant. And exactly how free are addicts to overcome their addiction? How free are any of us to change ourselves?

Cynthia realized her struggle against blurting out whatever came to mind was minor compared to opioid addiction, yet it was something she had to deal with relating to Justin. She couldn't slash and burn him whenever the impulse came to her acid tongue. She had to do better than that. She needed to say what she needed to say with respect. Justin knew how to steel himself against his mother's unfiltered utterances. Cynthia knew she didn't want him to steel himself, distance himself against her raw comments, her cutting remarks. Even in these early days of their marriage, Cynthia knew that.

Browsing through a bookstore, Cynthia found a book that spoke powerfully to her, *The Spirituality of Imperfection: Storytelling and the Search for Meaning* by Ernest Kurtz and Katherine Ketcham (1992). The book brings more than one-hundred stories from Hebrew prophets, Buddhist sages, Christian teachers, ancient Greeks to the modern insights of Alcoholics Anonymous. She brought the book with her when she came to see her dad and Dee.

Dee flipped through the book, read bits and pieces, and said, "This book seems to speak neither science or logic, or mere commonsense practicality. It brings stories of mythical wisdom, which feeds the human soul."

Cynthia summarized a paragraph from the book about how we attempt to chemically-manipulate what we can't control. We take medications to sleep, tranquilizers to dull nerves, alcohol to create sensations of warmth and belonging. But there is a vast difference between naturally falling asleep and lapsing into coma, between true relaxation and numbness, between being euphorically boozed-up versus the warmth and comfort of real relationships. We try to control with chemicals what is beyond our control and merely create a vicious cycle.

Cynthia wanted to control her tongue, for Dee had recently shared more than she ever had with Cynthia about years of gender confusion. Cynthia desperately did not want to blurt that out for any reason, for she knew Dee was trusting Cynthia with this information to illustrate the value of Francine having talked about androgyny; Francine's helpful mobius band, psychiatrist Carl Jung's regard for the feminine side of a male and the masculine side of a female (anima and animus) Dee's connection to the two sides of the brain tied to the history of Western Culture largely through Iain McGilchrist's book, *The Master and His Emissary.*

Dee talked about the tension of the opposites as well as complementarity present in seeming opposites. And again, Dee related in Genesis (1:26-27), "Let **US** make man in **OUR** image, after **OUR** likeness . . . So God created man in his own image, in the image of God he created him; male and female he created them." Dee could not let go of this bible passage. She felt confident that learning more about how these words have been interpreted throughout the ages might bring greater understanding to gender issues today.

Cynthia was grateful she'd grown-up in a household of mental stimulation. These days her dad was into the work of American historian David McCullough, feeling history currently was not dealt with enough gravity in the general population. Zach presently had two favorite history quotes. The first, by historian McCullough, "Nothing ever had to happen the way it happened." To Zach, these words place human choice at the center of history. Consciousness and choice walk hand-in-hand. The choices we make depend on our consciousness, our awareness, our mental-emotional frame of reference, our experiences, our personal and ancestral history, the depth and breadth of each human's horizon, as he'd been brainwashed by Dee, he suggested, in jest.

The second quote is David McCullough quoting another historian, ""Trying to plan for the future without a sense of the past is like trying to plant cut flowers." Zach found this sentence profoundly clever, abundantly wise. Cut flowers planted in soil won't grow. Both of these quotes were in a speech historian McCullough gave in 2005.

Zach shared his quotes with Dee and Cynthia. That day upon leaving Dee, Cynthia hugged Dee in a most heartfelt way. Cynthia was maturing in her appreciation of Dee while Dee was herself experiencing a growth spurt.

CHAPTER FORTY-SEVEN

"Our Lady of Tenderness"

Dee and Oriana talked at length about the Holy Trinity, an abstraction which held little profound meaning for Dee until now. She now comprehended Jesus as long anticipated, awaited Messiah, divinely-inspired fully-evolved human who walked the earth around 2,000 years ago and brought a shift of consciousness; divine energy available to humans, labeled Holy Spirit. Jesus the Christ (the anointed One) and Holy Spirit are part of Total Being, Beingness Itself, source of all that IS, which Dee now realizes as Father-Mother, Life-Source, Mother-Father.

Dee found herself less and less thinking, speaking, wondering about "God" and more about "The Holy Trinity" which describes a comprehensive realization of "God." She has had a paradigm shift, able to understand that The Holy Trinity might be considered the center of history rather than God, or Jesus, or Holy Spirit alone. Actually, the Holy Trinity is the composite momentum recognized in Christianity. She knew she was still on shaky ground with understanding the Holy Trinity.

Which in Dee's understanding meant: First, God as Androgynous Beingness, then shamanic Jesus the Christ, and then genderless Holy Spirit as abiding essence in history despite humanity's short-sightedness, incompleteness, limitations, in the second Genesis creation story, the story of The Fall. The Sacred Trinity alludes to Life-giving potential despite human limitation, stupidity, or atrocity.

Dee assumed there is more physical, psychological, moral/ethical, spiritual health than dis-ease on earth, though it is folly to ignore dis-ease and wrong-headedness, in all its forms. Perhaps the thrust of Trinitarian Truth covers all the bases, including all shadow elements in every situation; what people are in the dark about; situations that are more destructive than creative. Dee remembered Matti used baseball to talk about fourfold exegesis, whereas Dee used fourfold exegesis to re-cognize Jesus' parables.

Dee couldn't stop wondering if she might have come to grips with her gender confusion earlier if the Trinity of her youth had included Mother-Father, masculine-feminine, rather than exclusive male-identity. One might protest that the Holy Spirit is gender-free. However, isn't it more likely that the Holy Spirit throughout history has been referred to as "him or he" rather than as genderless.

At the recent Brunch Bunch gathering in Monique's home, Estelle talked again about her favorite icon *The Virgin of Vladimir*, also known as "Our Lady of Tenderness," the title preferred by Estelle, who summarized for her Brunch friends the crux of her current icon-gazing. **(Please see the black-and-white icon at the end of this novel).**

Estelle explained that the icon has been damaged by fires and plundering, also restored, though it is believed the faces of mother and child remain original. Then Estelle shared more of the fruits of her gazing, "The adult-child Mary holds, is me, my eyes steadfastly watching Mary, the Sacred feminine, far better for me than God the Father whom I never liked, just as my father the alcoholic I loved who was often unlikeable, while my mother was steadfast and wise, leading the family through daily storms.

"In the icon, the adult-child is me dressed in gold. Gold, which is an expression of my good fortune, "pure gold," to have experienced healing through psychological training as a high school counselor and through imagining of gospel stories in the Spiritual Exercises of Ignatius of Loyola. Yet, and yet, it is the Sacred Feminine that is too scarce in ways in "Holy Mother the Church," the Sacred Feminine I find in the rosary, the

Eternal Feminine surely in the first creation story in Genesis, which Dee shared with us, the Feminine side of life that I have personally experienced as strong, steady, abiding, through my earthly mother."

Estelle repeated, "The icon's adult-child is me, gazing at Mary. Me, pleadingly needy, seeking, searching, for guidance, for strength, for understanding, for help, for answers to living this life. Part of me believes the icon's adult-child should be Jesus held by Mary. But that is not the case as occurs to me and my gazing. I am the one in need, lovingly held by Mary, who is more approachable than God as Father. I keep the icon close at hand; move her from room to room. I easily relate to her."

Estelle shared what she's been wondering, worrying about these days. "I wonder if e-mailing Feldon is my overreaction to masculine attention paid to me. Really and truly, I was flattered by his attention, dove-tailing with widow loneliness, which sums-up for the moment my uncharacteristic behavior of e-mailing him because he suggested it. I remain open to seeing more about myself through this Feldon episode, which has left me feeling vulnerable."

Why had she e-mailed Feldon? It was unlike her to have contacted him. It was natural that widow's loneliness had prompted her to do this, she told herself, remembering Francine's mobius band highlighting traditional masculine-feminine approaches to the world, and remembering Oriana and Dee drawing of a spiral as the center of creating a meaningful life, from higher and broader perspectives. She told herself she felt emotionally vulnerable, which she didn't like. What was she learning in her spiral journey at this time? She wistfully concluded, "The children and grandchildren are my mainstays but they're all very busy. I would enjoy having a dependable friendship with a male."

CHAPTER FORTY-EIGHT

Oriana Competing with Monique

The Brunch Bunch was quiet, speechless, after Estelle's raw appraisal of her vulnerability with the icon and Feldon. Monique in blunt fashion broke the silence, "And your embarrassment about vulnerability and Feldon?" In her generous way, Estelle rescued the moment, "Yes, my embarrassment about feeling vulnerable, which I am almost too embarrassed to admit."

Monique seemed unfazed, "Remember in the winter I shared about Canadian Sebastian, who as Canadian winter thawed, so did interest in each other. We stopped e-mails. Our romance thawed like Canadian weather. I admit my embarrassment to tell you that."

Monique continued, "Mostly, however, I remain in love with paintings of Marc Chagall; which are icons to me," as she put her hand on the over-sized Chagall book opened to a painting on the low table next to her. "I gaze them with no rational comprehension—only emotional connection. Chagall grew up peasant, me too, with animals on my grandparents' farm, butchering, birthing, plants, beautiful nature in my veins, romantic passion, too, with Henri, which became terrible suffering. Tragedy. The world upside-down.

"Forever I remain peasant pretending to be successful real estate agent. Or, successful real estate agent hanging onto soulful peasant realities of land, sky, crops, animals, fresh foods, smells and sounds of church festivals and traditions. My children do not know peasant-me. They are urban Americans, married, so I am not first with them; their partners are first."

Monique brought the group to awkward silence again. Was mother-in-law Dee about to be snagged into discomfort by what Monique might say about the Justin-Cynthia marriage? Dee had noticed since the marriage of Cynthia and Justin that Monique seemed to avoid the reality of their marriage, as if she was tiptoeing around the fact to keep from making a regrettable remark. Should Dee now say something to keep Monique from tripping over her own tongue?

Monique kept talking, "Things were better before Francine died. Sebastian and me shared language, cultural roots. Now, both people with personal cultural bond to me, are gone."

Across the room sat Spanish-speaking Oriana, certainly not a replacement for French-speaking Francine, Monique might have been implying, who saved the perilous moment with her own humor, "Chagall's paintings, living most years in Paris, soothe, awaken, penetrate and pierce my soul; never embarrass me against myself, so I'm happy enough," as she flipped to another painting in the gigantic book.

Monique continued, "Chagall grew up Hasidic Jewish. Me, mystical Catholic; Eternal Reality in the background or foreground of a middle-ground life where I stayed obediently practical, functional, dependable, a fragment of time in timeless universe. Chagall's paintings lessen middle-ground heaviness, until death allows escape. I understand Henri's desperation. Chagall's colors and impractical impressions lessen harsh realities; bring airy, lighter, sublime renderings, humorous possibility I love. Chagall's dedication to giving eyesight to the unseen coincides with *wonderings* and *wanderings* inside me." Monique spelled the two "w" words to be sure everyone understood.

Puerto Rican born Oriana quietly assessed Monique: How could Monique have lived so long in the U.S. and not learned to speak better English? Perhaps eccentric Monique drew attention to herself speaking in such an incoherent way. Monique had limited education compared to

Oriana, which made Oriana feel momentarily superior. Was Monique's seeming affection for Chagall's art mere staging to boost her self-made image of a high-brow cultivated woman?

Oriana admitted to herself that Monique had more fashion sense than her own plainer, somewhat plumper self. However, it felt good knowing they both started out with peasant backgrounds, though Oriana would never have used that word to describe herself as Monique had done. Oriana would have said she grew up in humble circumstances in rural Puerto Rico.

Oriana saw that Monique could hold captive the attention of a few friends, whereas professor Oriana had routinely held the attention of a roomful of students. Oriana knew Monique's husband had divorced her, while Oriana's marriage was intact until her husband's death. Monique likely made more money than Oriana, however, Oriana was now retired with a more than adequate income, whereas Monique was still working, Oriana gloated momentarily.

Oriana realized she was comparing herself to Monique which sprung from feelings of inadequacy, inferiority, insecurity. Oriana was angry at Monique for treating the Puerto Rican like an imposter after Francine's death. Oriana did not have such uneasiness with Dee or Estelle, who were both born U.S. citizens, not immigrants.

But wait, Puerto Ricans have been U.S. citizens since 1917! Oriana was born a U.S. citizen! She was losing her bearings in the vicious game of contrast and compare. She was shocked at what was going on inside her.

CHAPTER FORTY-NINE

Whole-Brain Christianity

Was this intense game of competition/comparison mere left-brain-hemisphere chatter triggered by emotion? Or was emotion triggered by this free-floating brain chatter? Where was the soul in this happening, this internal behavior? Well, of course, the soul is just an idea, nothing but an idea, not a physical reality like the brain, Oriana reasoned. The soul is an unprovable, though powerful idea, which includes the religious idea of an immortal soul.

But then, Oriana corrected herself: Just an idea? Nothing but an idea? People kill each other over ideas, differing religious ideas, clashing economic ideas such as communism, socialism, capitalism, competing political ideas such as democracy, fascism, totalitarianism.

Oriana felt unmoored, untethered by Monique's bold, chic demeanor, her impassioned presentation of Chagall's creations. Yet Oriana felt Monique's understanding of anything but juggling real estate was shallow. Or was this a projection? Was Oriana herself of shallow understanding? Was this her fear? Oriana was aware she was pretending to listen with interest to Monique while embroiled in her own thoughts.

Just then, Oriana saw Monique wipe away a tear on her cheek with the back of her hand, and heard her say, "Christiane and Jameson moving out from the house wrench me. Justin's quick wedding, Francine's death, Christiane's wedding unnerve myself. I am alone. I open Chagall's book of paintings, enter myself into colors and shapes created by a human, piercing depths of my essence I do not understand.

"Too long Henri is gone. We had love together, but his weakness more powerful than my strength. Here Chagall shows romantic love," as she displays his painting, *The Lovers of Vence,* 1957, making scattered observations about the painting, "I long for this," as she points to parts of the painting: "even now chest aches, arms yearn, my body desires embrace, here, the animal-sexual is close to sun energy, the clay earth, a small masculine head close at animal feet. Delicate flowers, colors reflected in male-figure. Blue trees, green purview. Green nature, green as in immature, (green behind the ears). Henri and I were beginning sprouts, healthy plantings. Human civilization in the background, buildings. Estelle, does Feldon hold no promise for you?"

Monique's free-wheeling monologue ended, shocking Estelle into startled response, "Oh, I don't know. Feldon and I would not be young lovers as are the two in the painting. We are both elders closer to burial in the clay of the earth of Chagall's painting, than in the fresh flowers held by the young couple. City buildings in the center of the painting may depict human nature, humanity as builders, creators of culture. How do the elderly amongst us view today's culture compared to when we were in our physical prime? How might the painting change for you if the lovers were two older people?"

Monique seemed momentarily speechless, beside herself. She did not answer Estelle's question about two older lovers. Instead, Dee introduced with a dash of humor, making fun of herself, an expected suggestion, "What if the two lovers symbolize the brain hemispheres, united rather than competing. Is that an inspiring interpretation?"

Monique's attention returned, "Chagall would not paint the brain. He is real, actual." Dee, in an unusual mood goaded Monique, "The brain is real, just hidden inside the head." Dee further teased, "If Chagall can paint red farm animals, flying pigs, why not the human brain in the form of two lovers?" Dee then realized the degree of Monique's fragility dealing with loneliness, new living arrangements, change, and Dee gently retracted, "I understand what you're saying, Monique."

Monique was not about to let go of Chagall's creations, their inexplicable hold on her. She turned to the end of the huge book, and carefully read sentences, not consecutive sentences, but some she'd carefully pieced together, explaining the effect of Chagall's paintings on her.

"To someone who likes Chagall's art, his creations are water to a person dying from thirst . . . In this day and time, too much rational science, too much practical, technical progress. Chagall has freedom of imagination. Imagination is spiritual reality. Without imagination spiritual reality loses power. . . Today, an imbalance of shallow rational . . . Chagall brings deep soul to help cure today's domination imbalance."

The room was quiet until indomitable Monique spoke, "Could be that addicts, whatever kind, in love with Chagall paintings, ingest them, get filled by true fullness—if they accept flying farm animals, blue pigs," she looked at Dee with good humor—and then continued, "Humans have soul dis-eases. Chagall's mythical creations help heal my soul."

The eyes of Dee and Oriana met when Monique said the words 'mythical creations,' recalling their recent conversation on popular culture's giants, scientism and rationalism, as straight arrows compared to the myth of a spiral at the center in a soul's journey. Liberating truth is more like a spiral than an arrow. The soul revisits situations, topics, issues, again and yet again at greater levels of awareness. This is growth, transformation, evolving.

Oriana and Dee were stunned by similarities between Monique's quotes about Chagall's paintings in the oversized book and the conclusion in their own talk of a spiral journey. Both her quotes about Chagall and their spiral sketch point beyond current culture's hermeneutic horizon to a more whole hermeneutic coming alive.

Dare Dee tie the idea of the soul to the right-brain-hemisphere? No, that would be to concretize soul too much, she decided. Yet, put soul in terms of whole-brain Christianity in this postmodern time, in the retrieval and renewal of what Christ Jesus brought to earth to replenish the human soul, then mention of right-brain-hemisphere might be helpful to glimpse and magnify the practical significance of soul, the mystical, mythical soul.

The term 'Whole-brain Christianity' might help Christianity today re-formulate itself, re-theologize, expand its hermeneutic horizons.

Oriana admitted to herself that Monique's statements had perhaps sharpened her understanding of Chagall's soulful envisionings, as a kind of Deep calling to Deep. While Monique was hoping she'd been sufficiently clear to impress former professor Oriana.

At this very moment, Estelle remained stricken by Monique's question, "Does Feldon hold no promise for you?"

CHAPTER FIFTY

Numinosity and Projection

Estelle was turning mental cartwheels regarding Feldon. She was intrigued by him. In his most recent e-mail, he suggested they have coffee together. They had not yet been out together. Only e-mailed. However, Reggie had departed this life only little more than a year and a half. She didn't know how she felt about any of this.

She didn't know how her children would view this, or her sisters. She'd had conversations with her sisters about the inadvisability of elder-romance. Her one sister was widowed and said she wouldn't want to care for another person as she had for her husband before he died, nor would she want a spouse to care for her in that way. Estelle was acutely aware of her own aging, and not at all sure she wanted to share the process intimately with another.

Yet, Feldon seemed an interesting conversationalist, which was important to her. She had a widowed friend from years past, around Estelle's age, who remarried a few years ago and explained the decision to remarry not as being in love, but as both she and her new husband having admitted to one another that each was lonely after their spouses died. Estelle's friend and new husband moved away, and Estelle lost contact with her and therefore didn't know how the marriage turned out.

Estelle knew what she wanted was friendship, enduring friendship with a male, but no marriage, no living with someone, no legal ties. She needed two independent households. And here she was dredging up all these possibilities, scarcely knowing Feldon, realizing she liked being by herself, alone, spending time alone, despite sometimes feeling lonely. And yet, if a meaningful friendship was available, shouldn't she embrace it?

Several days ago, Dexter, Estelle's 19-year-old grandson telephoned to chat. She'd had a knee-jerk reaction when she noticed he was calling, worried there might be some difficulty. But no, Dexter was primarily concerned with death, how when someone dies, they are really gone. She felt he was referring to his grandfather Reggie's death, the first family death Dexter had experienced.

Dexter said he'd started wanting to use each day to its fullest, because who knew whether he would have a short life or a long one. The two of them talked about time and timelessness. For a while now he'd been wanting to someday make videos that awaken humanity to something ultimate, for which he was still searching.

For the first time Estelle could remember, Dexter said he "has a lot to learn" about things, the way life is. He admitted having a lot to learn living in an apartment with a guy roommate, taking college classes, having a part-time job in a restaurant, grateful for the financial support of his parents. He further commented he was learning about the good and not so good parts of the relationship with his girlfriend.

Estelle felt Dexter was maturing and she could empathize with his struggles as well as the exciting elements of everyday life. She was overall amused that she was wondering (concerned) about coffee with Feldon. In a way, she was at the same level as Dexter and his girlfriend, and she smiled at the similarity. Estelle sorely missed the times she and Reggie spent with Zach and Dee.

The best investment the Kendricks made was buying the dual recliner where they sat together, shared ideas, watched television, sometimes read; just sitting close together was satisfying, fulfilling, tender, intimate.

Dee and Zach were talking about *numinosity*, which isn't exactly an everyday word. It has to do with experiencing something out of the ordinary. Numinosity is a combination of fascination, wonder, awe, mystery, intuitive knowing, exalted awareness.

Dee read about childhood ecstatic experience, and wondered about the numinous becoming squelched and lost by the time one is an adult. And why might the capacity for rapturous awareness get choked? Dee concluded adults become too left-hemisphere oriented, trusting only in five-sense reality, getting crushed by responsibilities and so rushed with duties that there is no time for timelessness, the eternal, to break through. When this happens to us, we learn to fear, she concluded.

This includes fear of non-rational events, fear of anything beyond the material five-sense world, fear about survival, fear about paying the bills, a fear-ridden relationship to time which results in feeling driven or plunging us into paralyzing procrastination, or into the paralysis of analysis. It is said, 'Perfect Love casts out fear.' It is perfect love we seek which is always seeking us. She found uplifting the idea of being sought by Perfect Love. Just thinking about Perfect Love seeking us is helpful when burdened as an adult.

Children do not yet fear experiencing the unknown, for most everything is still largely unknown to us as children. Children are open and receptive to what happens next. However, growing-up demands that we learn to keep schedules and perform dutifully. We become more and more left-hemisphere oriented. The right-hemisphere childhood ability to live in the moment, enamored with being alive, fades.

Dee, an early riser, went most mornings to the back-yard to bask in the freshness of a new day, to keep in touch with nature. She was enamored with sky, sunrise, sunsets, moon and stars, rainbows, the breeze, wind, air. She noticed the side of a breakfast cereal box which reminds us we ingest phosphorus, magnesium, iron, zinc, copper, elements of the earth itself. Staying connected with nature feeds us in many ways.

Rituals nourish us; traditional religious rituals as well as ordinary events. Shower or bath can be a sacred ritual, a time of prayer, meditation, a time of cleansing soul and body; the same for jogging, working out, going for walks, walking the dog. These can be psycho-spiritual exercises as well as physical ones. Adults can easily under-use the imagination. Play, stories, games, chatting, laughter, with no purpose other than to enjoy and delight, feed us. Pets and children can help adults recover and retain this side of themselves.

In our left-hemisphere highly-competitive, success-driven, goal-oriented, time-urgent culture it's not hard to lose childhood capacity for experiencing the divine, the sacred, the holy, the numinous. Is it any wonder that addictions and compulsions are commonplace attempts to fill our yearning for what is intimately ultimate.

Depression runs rampant when the wellsprings of life run dry; when psycho-spiritual drought sets-in. Parched, we begin living in an interior desert, seemingly deserted by that which alone can quench our thirst, our longing to intimately, personally, profoundly experience being Life's much-loved child.

We often don't feel like Life's much-loved child. Everyone needs to be salvaged in one way or another. And, indeed, the world is salvaged, healed, transformed, "saved" one person at a time. Recovering the functions of the right-hemisphere of the brain is part of the healing that Christianity needs. The right-hemisphere more often than the left generates feeling-states. Blaise Pascal wrote that when a person experiences love or ecstasy, he or she knows it. One doesn't forget a numinous experience.

Perhaps it is true that one doesn't forget numinous experience. However, an adult who has largely abandoned right-hemisphere experience may begin unconsciously, unknowingly, searching for numinosity. Such an individual may study and train to become clergy hoping thereby to ensure numinous experience, contact with God, being made whole in God's love. When this does not happen, the personality may be stymied, disappointed, unfulfilled, but the original longing for numinosity remains. This is when a projection is likely to occur. A projection is the psychological term which explains why we sometimes have emotionally-charged positive attractions (romantic attraction) or negative revulsions (annoyance and irritation) to people, places, things.

Dee wished every person on earth understood projection. For instance, one may find a movie enthralling while another finds the same movie lackluster or boring. Different reactions are comments on one's personality, which doesn't mean every preference is a projection. Excessive emotion is the central feature of projection: this is when something grabs us emotionally because a vital aspect of our personality of which we are unaware is alerted, awakened, activated.

When something is projected, we see it as outside of us, as though it belongs to someone else and has nothing to do with us. We do not decide to project something, it happens automatically. Projection can be a psychological mirror. Projection happens when a person, place or thing reflects some part of our personality back to us and stirs-up emotional energy in us, positive or negative.

Depth psychologists say each time projection occurs there is an opportunity to learn something vital about oneself. Paying attention to what stirs within one's own personality reaps its own benefits of personal insight, self-knowledge, which is why Francine strongly believed romantic attraction is an opportunity to learn about oneself as much as it is finding a mate.

Why did Dee have the need to review this information so familiar to her?

CHAPTER FIFTY-ONE

Three Influencers

One fine fall evening, gathered on the Kendrick patio for a Saturday evening meal were Sherry and Quinn, Cynthia and Justin, Dee and Zach. The group exchanged memories of Francine sharing meals and interesting topics on the patio. The group conversation this lovely evening shifted to today's culture. Have we lost our way? How might culture be replenished? The discussion centered on finding voices in today's world that can help heal humanity at this time.

Psychotherapist Sherry suggested Jill Bolte Taylor as a healing voice. Taylor, Harvard-trained neuroanatomist, had a left-hemisphere stroke at the age of 37, from which it took eight years of rehab for her to recover. During her stroke she was aware as left-hemisphere functions stopped working, her right-hemisphere activity was evident to her, which was a blissful experience of oneness with the universe. There's a TED talk video on this.

Sherry emphasized, "Jill Bolte Taylor is a wonderful teacher. Her most recent book, released in 2021, *Whole Brain Living: The Anatomy of Choice and the Four Characters That Drive Our Life*, is a practical book which is a mix of neuroanatomy and psychology. This latest book draws the reader into information so usable and effective it helps change one's perspective without dogged effort or determination. The book brings a heap of liberating truth.

"Taylor is a delight to experience on internet videos, where she teaches about four characters we each have in our personality and how they affect the choices we make. My clients benefit from watching her videoes. She brings commonsense wisdom to today's often jumbled world. She's a voice of profound sanity easily available on the internet. Having suffered a stroke, struggled through eight years of rehab to recover, she's believable as few people can be. Taylor is a voice who has much to offer for our time. I find her a voice of hopeful contribution."

Dee laughed at what she was about to say, for it was so predictable, "A voice that has helped bring sanity to me is Iain McGilchrist. I nominate him as a current voice to help heal culture." The group was amused at Dee's choice. She gave a full description of him, knowing well, that the others already knew McGilchrist was a humanities professor at Oxford University and philosopher, before he became a psychiatrist, and then a master author on research related to brain-hemisphere differences and their impact on the world we create."

Dee continued, "McGilchrist writes ginormous books. His background in the humanities enables him to grasp life in a broader way than most, which I believe is why he has so much to say. His mammoth book, *The Master And His Emissary: The Divided Brain and the Making of the Western World* (2009), now as a new expanded edition (2019), is a gift to help us understand how we interpret ourself, others, and ultimately shape culture.

"McGilchrist, featured in many, many internet videos, explains how in his books he uncovers, expands, defines and refines right-hemisphere traits and qualities, which have been traditionally been overshadowed by overvalued left-hemisphere preference. The right-hemisphere has been regarded as contributing little, or close to nothing, to the way we experience the world.

"His latest book has just been released in two volumes. I haven't yet read it. *The Matter With Things: Our Brains, Our Delusions, and the Unmaking of the World* (2021)."

Justin interrupted and repeated, "The Unmaking of the World?"

Cynthia questioned, "Our Delusions?"

Zach, well informed by Dee's profound interest in McGilchrist's ideas, could only ask another question, "Wouldn't you say it often feels as if we are today unmaking our world; maybe we are delusional? Delusion is a belief or impression that is persistently held contrary to a reasonable view of reality." Zach humorously looked at Dee for confirmation his definition of delusion was accurate.

She blinked her eyes, nodded her head, in exaggerated agreement with Zach, and added, "McGilchrist makes it ever clearer we have been living with the delusion that left-hemisphere contributions to our way of seeing the world are far superior to whatever the right-hemisphere has to offer."

Justin questioned further, "McGilchrist gives plenty of reason to think we are being culturally delusional?"

Dee could only say, "Yes, certainly in his book *The Master and His Emissary,* and I haven't read his two new volumes, but I feel primed for what more he has to say about this, for amongst his many videoes on YouTube I've watched, he's read introductions to his new two-volume *The Matter With Things,* and talked a great deal about this latest two-volume book of his.

"I suggest McGilchrist is a voice already being heard around the world. It is his work that makes me feel whole-brain Christianity can become a reality when enough people grasp what he is saying about brain-hemispheres and apply his insights to historical trends in Christianity over the centuries and certainly to today's Christianity."

Cynthia looked at dad-Zach and knowingly teased, "So, you also are a fan of McGilchrist as a healing voice on the horizon today? He refined her comment, "I greatly admire what I know about him, but have my own favorite idea-person, Rupert Sheldrake, who I find a fascinating voice. He's a research scholar with many talks on the internet, educated at Cambridge, a botanist and cell biologist, a scientist who lived and researched rain forest plants in Malaysia, and in India developed new cropping systems now widely used by farmers. In India he lived at the ashram of Fr. Bede Griffiths, a British Benedictine Catholic priest. Sheldrake is bold, broad, courageous, in his ideas, his research, his spiritual ideas.

"He developed the idea of morphic resonance, which is the process of an individual organism inheriting collective memory from past members of the species which affects other members of the species in the future.

"Some find Sheldrake too far out, too unconventional. I find him a breath of fresh air. Two very readable books of his are on spiritual practices: *Science and Spiritual Practices: Transformative Experiences and Their Effects on Our Bodies, Brains, and Health* (2017). *Ways To Go Beyond: And Why They Work* (2019). Each book deals with seven spiritual practices. Sheldrake's fourteen spiritual practices may surprise some.

"I say Christianity today probably needs shaking-up, since many have stopped going to church, apparently not being fed by what they find there. I am one of these. Or maybe not." The group quietly absorbed Zach's talk about Rupert Sheldrake. Then it was Cynthia's turn.

CHAPTER FIFTY-TWO

Another Healing Voice

Cynthia began, "Well, because of my father, but actually on my own, I learned a bit about Rupert Sheldrake, but mostly about his wife, Jill Purce, who I find is literally a healing voice for the world today. She has been teaching overtone chanting for decades. I've always wondered what Charles finds in chanting, and have never understood how hearing monks chanting changed the life of philosopher Simone Weil.

"And now I find Purce, who wrote the 1974 book *The Mystic Spiral, Journey of the Soul* (reprinted 2007), holds workshops where chanting is combined with healing family—ancestral, generational healing—wherein by attending to past generations, present and future generations are affected. This is my understanding. Purce seems a compelling spokesperson for what she has learned over decades of overtone chanting as spiritual practice combined with healing generational trauma, pain, suffering, damaged potential. Her newer and older interviews are on the internet.

"I remember Francine saying psychiatrist Carl Jung found too little attention was paid to generational considerations in psychotherapy."

Cynthia explained further, "Justin knows almost nothing about his father's side of the family. I suppose this fact sparked my newly-acquired

interest in what Purce does." Cynthia immediately felt she should, perhaps, not have brought Justin into what she said. However, he seemed
OK with what Cynthia said, and added, "In therapies I've been in, generational issues have been brought up. If I could attend a chanting work-
shop that would shed light on my own ancestry, I'd do so."

Psychotherapist Sherry found Justin's remarks interesting. She had
only recently heard of Purce's work through Cynthia and planned to learn
more. She prodded Quinn, "As a biology teacher, which of these voices
favored this evening, are you more likely to present to your students?"

He replied, "Let me first say Catholics routinely, traditionally pray for
those who have died, which doesn't mean more can't be understood
about this practice of generational healing—more dimensions incorpo-
rated into praying for the deceased, for deceased ancestors.

"As for brain-hemisphere differences, that information is already in
the material we use in class, so it's easy to include McGilchrist and Taylor.
I also bring up energy fields in class, so can easily include Sheldrake's
morphic resonance, morphogenetic field, and Purce's chanting and generational healing.

"Adolescent students have cognitive skills and open attitudes to ab-
sorb new possibilities better than most older people. I can bring these
ideas into my biology classes, and students would likely appreciate what
the ideas offer. Remember, our students are non-traditional in their approaches to knowledge and understanding, and tend to be open to new
perspectives."

Dee commented, "All four voices, Taylor, McGilchrist, Sheldrake,
Purce, deserve credit for writing, giving talks, which it seems to me, can
help revitalize culture should what they offer become commonplace in
the populace."

Sherry agreed, "I see how their work might bring Christianity to its
fullness—there could be whole brain Christianity—that possibility is very
real to me." Zach added, "Not only Christianity, but there might be
whole-brain religions, which the world needs. Many have been maimed
and killed in the name of religion."

Quinn thoughtfully, wryly questioned, "You are suggesting scientists,
non-theologians, those in the secular domain, will save Western Culture,
the whole world, from disintegration into fragmented, piecemeal

meaninglessness? These secular types will save the jobs of clergy and churches? Churches and clergy, the bastion of transcendent meaning, will be rescued by science and secular ideas?!" Quinn proclaimed this with exaggerated amazement, though the idea didn't seem strange or bizarre to anyone in the group, including Quinn.

The patio was quiet until Cynthia recalled, "Dee, do you remember a time Francine told about a Methodist clergyman who'd written years ago of a church building with steeple spires contrasted with a church with a dome, comparing the two sides of the brain?"

Dee nodded, "I do remember."

It was a memory Cynthia and Dee pieced together when Francine told of a theologian who took brain-hemisphere research in its early days and applied it to Western Christianity's Chartres Cathedral with spires poking dramatically into the sky outside Paris, compared to the massive domed church in Istanbul, St. Sophia (*Hagia Sophia*—Holy Wisdom—now a mosque) built by Eastern Christianity, and how he speculated the drastic dissimilarity between the churches' architecture reflected differences between Eastern and Western religious approaches.

The theologian concluded the God of Eastern Christianity was right-minded (mystical); the Western God left-minded (rational), and that Eastern and Western Christianity need each other to be whole. Francine had shared this story with the Brunch Bunch and again when Dee and Cynthia delivered fresh vegetables to her house.

This present special evening on the patio, Dee also remembered first learning about allusion confusion and metaphoric discernment from Ann Dramm. Little did she know practical hermeneutics would become her passion. The Texas Trio friends of Ann Dramm would open the door to a hermeneutic hobby, including the fourfold interpretation of Jesus' parables.

Further, Dee felt her hermeneutic hobby boosted her higher on the spiral of learning, psychological insight, spiritual growth and development—the spiral she and Oriana often sat with these days.

That evening on the Kendrick patio, Cynthia and Dee pieced together their mutual memory of Francine talking about brain-hemisphere contrast related to church architecture. Their pleasant exchange was evidence of Cynthia's more respectful, mature behavior toward Dee. In that memory of Francine they experienced themselves as allies—on the same wavelength—in a compatible mindset. Overall, the evening was drenched in compatibility, with family and friends enjoying their togetherness.

CHAPTER FIFTY-THREE

Soul-Satisfying Evening

After guests left the patio that special evening of compatibility, Zach and Dee playfully evaluated the evening, using Dee's fourfold hermeneutic. They counted food, drink and even the weather, as lovely creature comforts for physical enjoyment, pleasure. Joyful serenity seemed to have reigned psychologically within each person. Loving conduct, interactions, behaviors, were present, fulfilling the moral/ethical exponent.

As for the spiritual aspect of the fourfold hermeneutic, Dee and Zach decided the cosmic life source, divine grace, permeated, saturated the event, the evening, the overall happening, which was ever so fine. There was this quality about the evening.

The hosts laughed at their folly as they rated the evening "sublime." Their experience of this special evening, they labeled "soul satisfying." As if, in this place, at this time, with these people, the best was experienced. The evening was so fine it was as if heaven and earth merged, which was indeed sublime.

Life in Sandshell and the nation was recovering from Covid-19's social distancing. Human activity was emerging to greater fullness. To be specific: Sherry and Quinn married. The relationship between Cynthia and Sherry blossomed again into what it had been. Couples Cynthia and Justin, Sherry and Quinn, liked one another; enjoyed activities together. The husbands alongside Zach came to enjoy golf. The Brunch Bunch continued, thanks to Dee's original initiative, and her recognizing the on-going need for friendship. Monique and Oriana developed a special fondness between them. Estelle and Feldon became committed friends. Little Pixie-Pickett and big Bios played together with reckless abandon whenever they had the opportunity. The Kendrick patio continued to be a gathering place of in-depth conversation.

The Virgin of Vladimir
also known as
"Our Lady of Tenderness"

ACKNOWLEDGMENTS

Special thanks to Maureen Lumley, PhD, who connected the author with Jennifer Leigh Selig, PhD, publisher of Empress Publications.

And Mary Fernandez, thank you for connecting the author to the icon.